One Good Road Is Enough

ALSO BY ROBERT WALLER

Just Beyond the Firelight:
Stories and Essays by Robert James Waller

One Good Road Is Enough

ESSAYS BY **ROBERT JAMES WALLER**

IOWA STATE UNIVERSITY PRESS / AMES

Some of the essays in this book have previously appeared in the *Des Moines Register, Country America, Humane Society of the United States News, League Lines,* and *Voice of Humanity.*

Manufactured in the United States of America
♾ This book is printed on acid-free paper.

First edition, 1990
Second paperback printing, 1990

Library of Congress Cataloging-in-Publication Data

Waller, Robert James
One good road is enough : essays / by Robert James Waller, – 1st ed.
p. cm.
ISBN 0-8138-1881-8 (alk. paper). – ISBN 0-8138-1880-X (pbk. : alk. paper)
I. title.
AC8.W266 1990
081 – dc20 90-4720

For John Warfield, my friend and colleague, whose brilliance, concern for making democracy work, and passion for truth are unmatched. In his own way, he taught me what someone else (I think it was Blaise Pascal) once said: There is light enough for those who wish to see and darkness enough for those of the opposite disposition.

Contents

Foreword

Robert Waller is a romantic. He sees and hears and feels things that most of us don't notice. He can find meaning in a high flight of geese coursing south, beauty in a mundane business transaction, and truth in the damnedest places. Even his darkest moments are lighted by the dry wit of a man thoroughly enjoying life.

I knew none of this when we first met in 1983. I was editor of the editorial pages of *The Des Moines Register* then, and on the theory that Iowa is endowed with a lot of bright people who have important ideas to share with others, I was combing the state for new writers for our pages. At lunch one day with some faculty members at the University of Northern Iowa in Cedar Falls, Jim Gannon (then the editor of the *Register*) or I—Waller and I remember this differently—told Waller about my quest, and Waller said he'd think about sending us a piece.

My hopes weren't great. Waller, in his splendidly tailored three-piece suit, had talked enthusiastically about some program the school was starting, his language full of the jargon and speed-talk that business professors seem to use when confronted by uncertainty. I figured he'd send me a musty piece on why business colleges are the last, best hope of civilization—and how UNI wasn't getting the credit it deserves—but I began to wonder later in the day when I mentioned Waller to Jack Hovelson, the *Register* reporter in Waterloo–Cedar Falls.

"Oh yeah," said Hovelson, "the basketball player." "No,"

I said, "the dean of the business college." "He was a basketball star," said Hovelson. "Well, he isn't very tall," I said. "You don't have to be when you've got the jump shot he had," said Hovelson.

Variations of that conversation have been happening to me ever since: "You mean the folk singer." "Oh, the canoeist." "The song writer." And I know now that a lot of other variations are available: the pool player, the consultant to Saudi Arabia, the photographer, the scholar, the conservationist, the poet, the spouse of ceramic artist Georgia Waller.

A few months later, Waller sent us an essay—the story of his days as a guitar player on Bobby Kennedy's 1968 whistle-stop campaign through Indiana—and we've been publishing his physical and intellectual meanderings ever since. This collection is his second, and I believe, like the first, it will be in print for many years to come.

People in journalism generally believe and find solace in the idea they are producing literature on the run. But the vast bulk of what they do is ephemeral, as fleeting as a mayfly, because they're seeking facts instead of truth. Robert Waller's quest is truth. He has no fear of where the facts will take him. It's a quality that most adults, in the charades that adults are wont to play, dismiss as childlike. Waller isn't afraid to show his feelings over a miserable little bird, he isn't afraid to challenge the hypocrisy of big-time college athletics, he isn't afraid to show his emotions and tell his secrets, and that gives his work a fundamental honesty that distinguishes literature from a cacophony of words.

I once tried to hire him for the job I now hold—editorial page columnist—and, beyond the obvious reason of his potential for making the rest of us look bad, I'm glad he didn't take the job. While he could easily master the form, I realize now that asking Waller to accept the discipline of writing in time and space would have been akin to caging a splendid beast that's meant to roam when and where its fancy takes it.

Prodded on by a north Iowa friend whose Celtic genes distrust any sentiment that doesn't come from his own heart, I still dismissed Robert Waller for a long time as a person dominated by fear, a person who does some things well but who walks around under a dark cloud that makes him afraid to try things he doesn't excel at. But his writing has demonstrated his fearlessness. As a matter of fact, I now doubt that he fears anything.

He simply isn't one who gives himself over to flip characterization or two-bit analysis. Bob Waller's equally at home slumping in a Main Street beer hall in north Iowa, sitting in a snobbish restaurant in Manhattan where he up-snoots the waiter by ordering a "Bud," singing Cole Porter, Willie Nelson, or his own quite-good stuff, walking in the teeming streets of Calcutta, talking at the lectern of a heady business seminar, squatting in his backyard to photograph a violet, or taking his graduate students to an art museum to demonstrate a point in the craft of management.

As readers of his essays find, that barely touches the surface of Waller's quest to know himself and the world around him and certainly doesn't do justice to his gentle suggestions on how to make this planet a better place by saving what we haven't destroyed.

In the foreword of Waller's first book, his friend Scott Cawelti, a University of Northern Iowa English professor and first-rate essayist, had this to say: " 'Multi-faceted' seems too tame, as does the now-trite 'Renaissance man.' I've come to see Robert Waller's character as a large old home with a room for practically every taste and interest."

I can't improve on that. But I can add that Robert Waller has lived where most people only dream of living and he has dreamed where most people only live. That gives his writing a richness that leaves you wanting more from him.

JAMES FLANSBURG

Preface

Twenty-four months ago, almost to the hour, I wrote the preface to my first collection of essays. Working mostly on weekends and late in the afternoon, when my day-job is finished, I didn't think I'd have another set of pieces ready by now. But, somehow, the ideas turned into articles and the speeches into essays, and I'm sitting here looking at two computer diskettes containing about 300 pages of manuscript.

In many ways, this second book is a continuation of the first one. If you read and liked *Just Beyond the Firelight,* which now is in its third printing, you'll probably feel the same about this collection. I think my ideas on the environment and our treatment of it are a little sharper here, and you'll notice that in several of the pieces I have taken some new chances with the language and with the laying bare of my own psyche. In general though, I continue in my attempts to run down and collar a slippery and shifting universe, and that's what you'll find in these pages.

As before, Bill Silag, Assistant Director and Chief Editor at the Iowa State University Press, kept me going. He's a fine, passionate cheerleader, which, of course, is one of the functions of a good editor. And there are the letters. They come from Richmond and Yakima and New York and Florida and California and Texas and other places. And, they come from the Iowans who write me long, thoughtful notes about their lives and our times. I have many friends out there in Iowa and in America that I didn't have a few years ago, and I treasure that.

Eleven of these essays have appeared previously in the *Des Moines Register.* I owe much to James Flansburg, who recently has switched from Editor of the Editorial Pages to columnist, for his advice and willingness to consider my work over the years.

In addition, other publications were kind enough to reprint several of the essays after they appeared in the *Register.* "A Matter of Honor" appeared in *Country America* magazine. "I Am Orange Band" was published by the *Humane Society of the United States News, League Lines* (the bimonthly publication of The League for Animal Welfare in Cincinnati), and *Voice of Humanity* (the quarterly publication of the Humane Society of Wichita County, Texas). "Southern Flight" also appeared in the *Humane Society of the United States News.* I sincerely appreciate the interest of these publications in the articles.

Finally, two of the articles from *Just Beyond the Firelight* have appeared in other places, and since I have no other means of doing it in public, I'll express my thanks here. *America West Airlines Magazine* published "A Rite of Passage in Three Cushions," and "A Canticle for Roadcat" appeared in *Cat Companion.*

Shirley Koslowski, of Waterloo, continues to read much of my work in draft form and provides tough criticism and helpful suggestions. The first is easy to find. The second is almost nonexistent. I may have read a particular piece ten times after writing it, but Shirley finds flaws or strengths or a better word in a certain spot than *Roget's* was able to provide. I thank her for that, particularly for her periodic note across the top of a manuscript that says, "This isn't Waller!"

Marilyn Keller, Assistant Managing Editor of the Iowa State University Press, edited the manuscript in a thorough and thoughtful fashion. She saved me from possible embarrassment in a number of places, and the book is much improved because of her work.

So, as always, it's been a group effort. The editors, the publishers, the readers, the critics, the writer–all of us move together in some kind of strange and intricate dance to produce writing. I hope the dance continues.

ROBERT WALLER

December 1989

One Good Road Is Enough

The Turning of Fifty

In my late forties, I came quartering down the years and forgot how old I was. When asked to give my age, I would run a quick cipher: "Let's see (mumble, move lips slightly) . . . born in . . . present year . . . subtract. . . ." Was this a simple inattentiveness caused by the distractions of a busy life, I wondered? Or maybe, I wondered again, if some winsome sleight-of-hand by the mind itself was at work, the balming of harsh reality by a man growing older.

In any case, others noticed it first. My turning fifty, that is. A few months before my birthday, people started speaking to me in peculiar tongues, saying things such as "Hey, hey, Bob-O, the BIG ONE's coming! How are you going to celebrate it?" "I'm too busy to have a birthday," I countered, shuffling away from the subject.

That was not good enough. Indeed, I was told, this is a seminal occasion and deep, indelible markings should be tooled upon the hours of August 1. So, when pressed, I would claim the day to be mine alone and declared I would spend it sloshing around in some quiet swamp with my cameras.

But I dawdled, made no plans, and others kindly took over. My friend, Scott, organized a small birthday party held two days before the actual date. Old friends were generous enough to attend, I sat in a lawn chair with red balloons tied to the back of it, and Scott took a class picture. That was as wild as it got. We had a genuinely good time, in a quiet way, and the affair fit my approach to things. Well, the balloons seemed a little out of character for me, but I thought afterwards that everyone ought to spend at least one day a year sitting in a chair with balloons tied to the back of it.

I drove the sixty miles up to Rockford the evening before my birthday and took my mother out for dinner. Lifting my glass as she lifted hers, I grinned, "Thanks for getting me here." She smiled back, said she was proud of me, and told me again how the delivery took place in the middle of an Iowa thunderstorm and how the hospital lights failed just before I was born. I leave the significance of those latter two events open to various interpretations.

On the day itself, I put aside my low-fat, semivegetarian tendencies and ate two Maid-Rites. That was rather like an act of homage to my youth. For it was in Roger Dixon's Charles City Maid-Rite where I first lunched as a young boy, and I have retained a nearly religious zeal for the loose-meat sandwiches since then. As part of this, trips to Des Moines often are scheduled in such a way that a stop at Taylor's Maid-Rite in Marshalltown is not only possible, but inevitable.

There are, you see, few rituals more sublime than slowly spinning back and forth on a counter stool and watching sandwich makings being scooped from the steam table of a true Maid-Rite cafe. Truth in this case flows from a purity of undiluted purpose, a place where nothing other than Maid-Rites are served, except for the essential milkshake and graham cracker pie.

After the Maid-Rites, I took a nap, did my three miles on the road, read for several hours, and watched a movie. No "Over-The-Hill-Gang" T-shirts were purchased, no champagne was chilled, and bad jokes about getting older were avoided entirely. My wife wrote me a lovely note that said, "I'm short on words, but long on love," which I thought, apart from the sentiment, was a model of good writing and deserved a steel guitar lick underneath it. She also gave me a small crystal embedded in silver made by a local craftsman, and upon the silver were etched a fish and a falcon to represent my love of things wild and free. That was it, and it was just fine.

Still, the gentle lash of my friends and relations about the day's significance had its effect. In the midst of my reading that afternoon, I began to drift, thinking about time and the curious spiral dance of which I am a part. If I am just one of a long file of travelers, how about the rest? What were they doing on some other August 1?

Galileo, for example, in 1633. In April of that year, the Church had forced him, under threat of torture, to recant the conclusions reached in his *Dialogue Concerning the Two Chief World Systems* that Ptolemy had been wrong and Copernicus had been right: earth was not the center of all things heavenly. So I imagined Galileo Galilei in Florence, afraid, angry, and alone on a warm August day.

How did a shepherd ranging over the hills of Sumer, 2,000 years before Galileo, feel on this day? Did the flutter of light and shadow cause him to stop and think of a woman in a nearby town or how life is passing strange? Was the Rev. Thomas Bayes working on his famous probability theorem on the first of August in 1760? The beauty of his proof, which is taken by some as the beginning of modern statistics, consistently has escaped my students.

And Socrates. Where was he on a fine August evening? Making his way home with other guests from a night at Xenophon's, I suppose. The music was fading, but there was yet enough wine in the blood to stir their tongues as they moved through the quiet streets of Athens, the conversation still lively, still centered around matters at the heart of things.

Was Alexander out on the desert with his armies? Where was Geronimo a hundred years ago? And how did the infantryman walking along the French hedgerows in 1944 feel? On some August 1st was Charlie Parker practicing scales in E-flat major and Gertrude Stein holding court in Paris and Dali twirling his moustache? Was Swinburne writing "The world is not sweet in the end" on my birthday somewhere in the cool of England, while a black woman stared through a haze of Alabama heat at distant rain clouds?

Swinging around in my chair, I looked at what surrounded me and imagined a future archeologist, perhaps some alien blob of magenta protoplasm, carefully brushing away the crust of five thousand years and making notes on what it found. "Computer keyboard—primitive method of data entry." "Guitar—well-preserved example of mid-twentieth-century instrument building." "Stapler—used for fastening papers together prior to the invention of laser bonding." "Camera—one of the last models predating portable, digital imaging."

Next, I reviewed my list of ways I do not want to die. For example, I have noted "In a hospital." And, "Tail-ended by a '74 Cadillac in front of K Mart while a blue-light special on men's underwear is commencing." Then I turned to the acceptable list. "Falling off a cliff in northern Iowa on a foggy morning while adjusting my tripod." Or, "A spear in the chest on the African veldt" (first preference).

I also remembered that, following his orders, the bones of Genghis Khan were carried about by his armies in the field after his death, as a kind of memorial. That's what morticians like to call "pre-need planning." Personally, I've always thought that Khan pushed things a bit, overstayed his welcome, as it were.

That was all good fun, but it took me no closer to anything fundamental than where I had been at the beginning. So I dug in a bit, started things running back and forth across the corpus callosum, and got down to basics, while the overhead fan turned slowly. "All right," I said to myself, "I'm gibbous, more than half-rounded, a long run from the chrisom and the breast. So what can be made of that? What do I know and feel here on a summer afternoon with a half-century stretching out in back of me?"

Ontologists searching for the meaning of existence generally leave me behind in their quest, at least in their writings. I suppose, as with other such matters, it would have helped to have been there, at the Café Flore with Sartre, de Beauvoir, and the rest when they gathered to deal with the foundations of being.

For me, I'm content with Waller's Second Conjecture: Existence takes on meaning only when you give it meaning by making it meaningful. And how do you make it meaningful? By listening to those almost-secret voices within you that, at certain critical times, whisper, "This is me."

In those moments, it's important to consciously note what you're doing and to do more of it, a lifetime of it, in fact. I think this is what Joseph Campbell means when he speaks of "following your bliss." In case this seems a little too narcissistic, a little too thin and self-focused, I also believe that the meaningful life must include a concern for things beyond yourself, including our animal friends, rivers, trees, and other humans.

For twenty years I have had the following verse by Bengali poet Rabindranath Tagore hanging above my desk:

> The song that I came to sing remains unsung to this day.
> I have spent my days in stringing and in unstringing my instrument.
> The time has not come true, the words have not been rightly set;
> Only there is the agony of wishing in my heart.

Those words have haunted me for two decades. And, as I move around, I think they apply to a fair number of people I meet. I now keep Tagore pasted above me more out of tradition than necessity. Somewhere, around forty, I began, though somewhat imperfectly, to get the instrument tuned, the words in order, and the melodies flowing. Ice skaters are required to learn school figures, basic stuff. Living is a little like that. You have to get the school figures down, get 'em cold, so you can execute them subconsciously.

When that happens, when the words began to flow and the melodies take shape, the search for meaning does not end, but life starts to become meaningful even as you seek to make it more that way. Others apparently get there earlier than I did. Many never do, and that is the great tragedy of our times and the failure of our civilization, for neither our religions nor our schools nor our informal social structures provide us with the tools to search, diligently, for meaning in this present life.

How do you know when you're getting there? Well, things feel right; there is a sense of unification, as if you are becoming a tapestry rather than a conglomeration of tangled threads, and you are doing the weaving yourself, almost effortlessly. Personally, I think the pursuit of trivia and rapacious, material acquisition so honored by this society thwart the search and inhibit the weaving, and that the arts are the prime vehicle for clarifying and accelerating the search. But that's another story for another time.

At some point, you have to deal with a hard and essential fact: you discover that the things you're good at and the things you love are not necessarily the same. Whatever wisdom I have, I tend to get much of it from strange places. One of them was an obscure film, *The Gig,* about musicians. A first-class professional is talking to a man who wants nothing more than to be a professional, but obviously cannot cut it. The pro is tired of the amateur's whining and obsequious pleas to join a band and says: "Music is not like religion; devotion is not enough." There it is. It's a good thing to know.

There's also the problem of doing away with the clutter. Like good composition of any kind, coming to grips with life requires a certain elegance of lifestyle, not in the sense of being fancy, but rather a consideration of what can be discarded in favor of simplicity. I propose there is an insidious plot to steal our time in the world we have created, and it's important to get rid of as many encumbrances as possible, including lawn care and excessive housekeeping. The sign my wife posted a long time ago says it rather nicely: "Today I Cherish, Tomorrow I Dust."

Even being a little antisocial helps. A friend of mine is fond of quoting something I said a few years back about my reluctance to attend events of borderline value: "You have fewer people at your funeral, but you get more reading time." There are krakens out there gobbling your life, and it's crucial that they be spotted and nullified.

Then there are the quantity people who want you to try and live forever. You've got to watch them, too. I'm not talking here about commonsense matters of diet and personal habits. I'm talking about those who resent flyers and do all they can to ground them. They're everywhere with cautious, chirping advice: "Keep your hands in the boat," "Hang on to the latchkey," "Stay away from the road." Some people see dragons all about them. Avoid those people and fight the dragons when they come along.

When you feel yourself starting to become whole, it's all right to accept positions of power, but not before then. The overriding problem with our country, and our world in general, is that we are, in large part, managed by incompetents. Most of these are men who have spent their lives seeking power rather than themselves.

Consequently, we are confronted with the grotesque spectacle of working for childish figures—half-baked little generals with overblown egos and no more understanding of the search for meaning than some primitive, base organism spending its time feeding on the lives and feelings of others, guzzling them up like strained peaches, cackling to themselves as they play shell games with other people's destinies.

Moreover, somewhere along the way, I think it's crucial

to deal with the damnable issue of mortality. There is, of course, the inevitability of it all—the end of life. As children, we are brought slowly to this understanding through events rather than introspection. A grandfather dies when you're eleven. It seems incomprehensible, at first.

But at the funeral parlor there are lowered voices and solemnity. The old man who was, more than anything, your friend lies there quietly. And it comes to you, maybe for the first time, that all of this is not unceasing. The first sense of loss is that of ice cream on Sunday mornings and the wonderful, atrocious lies with which he embellished the stories of his cowboy days. The second is more haunting: We are not everlasting.

So you begin to understand mortality, dimly though, and with a vague assuredness that it applies to others, but not to you. Around twenty-two, however, I endured what I call my "mortality crisis." For six months, almost involuntarily, I lay in bed at night examining the edges of my physiology, seeking peace with the tenuousness of it all. I lay there in the darkness, thinking and sweating, terrified at the prospect of my own death. That period was excruciating but healthy, I believe, for I determined that time and I should be wary allies, not opponents.

Then life gets busy, fears recede in the tumble of daily life. And nature helps in this. An inherent kindness exists in the process of aging. Except for the unforeseen miseries of homicide or wars or sudden catastrophic illness, we are allowed to move along gradually. Imagine, for a moment, that we looked and felt exactly the same at fifty as we did at twenty. But, then, on our fiftieth birthday, suppose we changed suddenly to the physical condition and appearance of, say, a ninety-year-old. That wouldn't work, psychologically. We graciously are given time to adjust. (Incidentally, I'm not denigrating the appearance of older people; I'm merely talking about change.)

In my bathroom mirror at home it works just this way. I see myself every morning. The changes are unnoticeable from day to day. But there are other reflections.

For the last ten years I have taught in an executive development program at the University of Richmond. I always visit there in June and am lodged in undergraduate student housing along with participants in the program. Such quarters are standardized, obviously, so even though I may shift from room to room over the years, the uniformity of the place provides the illusion that I am staying in the identical room each year.

This provides a benchmark of sorts. On each visit, scraping the shaving cream away, I have a chance to examine what twelve months have done to me. There is, I admit, a certain trauma connected with this annual experience. Yet, perversely, I also look forward to it as a kind of gruff and unforgiving timepiece, measuring my progress, telling the truth, refusing to lie.

And every June I am given over to marveling at the human capacity for handling the certainty of our own deaths, for writing our own obituaries even as we live. That we can comprehend our own demise and that we do not constantly whirl about in rabid frenzy at the thought of it is part of our magic, a built-in mechanism for sanity of the most powerful kind.

But the borders are there. They are stern and ineluctable, and I see them approaching. Clearly I see them, on summer mornings, as I stare at myself in the mirrors of Richmond.

Yet, there are voices that speak to me along the rivers, along the way. With scolding words, they counter the momentary sag born of distant mirrors and honest appraisal: "Saddle up, caballero, and stop sniffling." They are right, of course. When Odysseus cried, "There is nothing worse for men than wandering," he was correct in the metaphor but wrong in the physical reality. There are Yaqui drums in high-plains arroyos and ship engines north of Cairo I have not yet heard. There are beaches where you can still run naked at dawn and visions within a yard of my house that I have not yet seen through the lens of my Nikon.

I missed the last packet boat down the Missouri. It left from the Fort Lewis, Montana, levee in 1890. How I wish I had been on it, coming by places with names such as Malta Bend, just to have gathered in the sense of history and change that must have been stacked along the decks. But there are other boats. Some are Arab dhows with saffron-colored sails. They move through the waters of Ocean India, and I aim to sail upon such a boat along the Somali Current.

The voices of the river remind me that neither chemists nor alchemists can save me. And they tell me it's all right to remember, in Kipling's words, "That night we stormed Valhalla, a million years ago," that it's allowable to sing sweet lamentations for the death of blue autumns, but not to dwell upon those things entirely. For in the pleasant sorrow that comes from remembrance, time shifts in character. No longer an ally then, but a legendary bandit who'll steal your woman and take your passion and ride the evening train.

So the voices settle me. And I remember most of what I know that is good and true and lasting has come not from scholars but from minstrels and gypsies, from magicians and magic, from jugglers swallowing fire. It has come from small bands of travelers who followed the rivers and told me old stories and chanted old warnings of young women dancing through late afternoons and into the firelight, leaving only a footprint for the morning that follows.

Listening closely, then, I have learned that languor is not the price of serenity. I know there is more ahead of me than discounted airline tickets and shuffleboard, or a condo on the edge of a Scottsdale golf course. And, if it's all right with everyone else, I think I'll skip the midlife passage involving gold chains and Porsches and suntans.

Instead, I'm lacing up my 12-year-old Red Wings, loading the cameras, putting new strings on the 1957 Martin flattop, getting ready to go where egrets fly. Like an old rider of the surf, I can already see the next wave coming. It looks fine and fair. It looks worth the effort.

Incident at Sweet's Marsh

I can get excited about river otters. They not only look neat, they also are among those of God's creatures who take play seriously. If they were human, they'd probably live in California, drive Porsches, and have something to do with the entertainment business.

So it was that my heart fairly leapt when I read the announcement in the *Des Moines Sunday Register.* It said that twenty river otters would be released the following Wednesday at Sweet's Marsh, near Tripoli. I organized my week around that event, packed a sandwich and my cameras, and left for Tripoli early on a bright March morning.

I figured the crowd at the release would be small—a few people from the Iowa Department of Natural Resources with the animals and maybe a half-dozen other grizzled outdoor types. After all, I spend days along the rivers of Iowa without seeing anyone other than profiles in cars going over bridges.

When I pulled into the access to Sweet's Marsh, a man wearing a camouflage shirt said I should continue straight ahead for parking instructions. I always listen to men wearing camouflage shirts, no matter what they are telling me, so I continued on and parked behind eight other cars on the shoulder of the road. No one was there to provide parking instructions, so, as typical Iowans, we just worked it out for ourselves.

It was at this point I began to experience a slight twitching in my stomach, and it had nothing to do with the coffee in my thermos. You see, I never go to any place where parking instructions are required. That stems from multiple traumatic experiences I had as a child when Jaycees wearing pith helmets and waving canes used to direct traffic at the county fair. I began to associate parking instructions with crowds and noise and other assaults on my tender sensibilities.

By 9 A.M., approximately sixty people had gathered and were surrounding two small cages containing a few otters for public display. People stood around commenting about the animals' inherent cuteness and firing away with point-and-shoot cameras.

"Well, this isn't too bad," I thought. Then I saw the state trooper. I also never go to events where state troopers are required. Not because I don't like state troopers, understand. My experiences with them have been distant, but pleasant. It's just that the presence of a trooper meant that crowd control of a somewhat higher order might be required.

I moved off to one side, poured a little coffee into my cup, and considered it all. Meanwhile, the DNR folks were busy stringing rope barricades along the south side of the inlet where the otters would be released. I started adding it up: parking instructions plus state trooper plus rope barricades equals *uh oh*.

But I love otters and wanted to see the little folks out of their wire mesh cages and in the water. So I decided to grit it out. That was when the yellow school buses began to arrive, and I knew it was all over.

I absolutely never go anywhere that involves yellow school buses. Never. Unless I am paid, and paid handsomely, for it. But the buses came and purged themselves of their cargos. The running, jumping, shrieking future business leaders of America poured from the open doors, glands pounding. But, what the hell. It's better than another hour of Cooperative Living (For Seniors Only, Elective) taught from some smarmy textbook designed to kill creative passion once and for all.

The students ran to be in the front row behind the rope barricades. I ran to the north side of the inlet where I figured the swampy ground would discourage those in new Reeboks. No luck. I had merely broken the ice by being the first into that area. Another veteran of the rivers soon joined me, grumbling about what a mess this was turning out to be.

Then came a heavy-set guy pawing through the branches with a 35-mm camera equipped with at least a 14,000-mm lens. That not being enough, he had affixed a teleconverter between the lens and the camera, which increases the effective length of the lens. He was hand-holding the camera and lens and attachments. I lost track of him, but if he was able to avoid sinking in the lowland low and to lift the apparatus to eye level and fire, I can tell you what his pictures look like without seeing them. It's the way the world looks to someone who has just been hit sharply behind the ear with a tire iron.

More yellow school buses. Driven by the same drivers, of course. I finally sorted it all out a few years ago. There are only twelve school bus drivers in the whole world. That's why they all seem to look the same.

I staked out a couple of feet of ground, set up my tripod, and asked the ninth-grade boys behind me to please stop pushing each other into the tree branch that whacked me each time one of them fell against it. Why do ninth-grade boys always push each other? Why haven't we shipped them all to North Dakota until they calm down?

By this time, I knew exactly why the state trooper was there. He had a drawn and jaundiced look to him, a legacy of too many county fairs and otter releases. I estimated the crowd at four hundred, with more cars and buses still arriving. At 9:30, the promised time for the freeing of the otters, a Department of Natural Resources man with a new-age bullhorn got on top of a pickup truck and asked the crowd for its attention. Attention? He had to be kidding.

Then he started a spiel about otters and their habitat and how lucky we are to have seed stock that may result in a viable otter population in Iowa. He tried to point out that we used to have lots of otters, but that they were driven to extinction by pollution, loss of habitat, and yellow school buses.

His speech did not go well. It suffered the same problems as 98.73 percent of all other speeches—an inadequate sound system and length. It went something like this: "Baarraak . . . otters . . . (muffled words) . . . rrarkk . . . thanks to . . . kkkzzrrak."

He did manage somehow to get across that it would take decades before the otter population was large enough to "harvest." There's that word again! We persist in using the euphemism wherever the slaughtering of attractive animals is being talked about. Dammit, we kill them. We slaughter them, just like we slaughter cattle. We catch them in steel traps or blow them down with shotguns. We rip off their hides and wear their furs or hang their heads on den walls. We *kill them,* we don't *harvest them!* Someday we'll all grow up and face that reality.

The speech droned on and on, the crowd became restive. You could almost hear it under people's breath—a chant still in the mind but ready to spring forth if the speech continued. "We want the otters, we want the otters, we want. . . ." The state trooper stiffened, sensing the otter-release equivalent of a feeding frenzy.

But I don't blame the DNR people. Cripes, they spend most of their time in obscurity, working hard with seines and handling squishy, crawly things under an August sun. By jove, for once they had a crowd, and this was a chance for their message to get across, whatever it was.

While the speaker spoke, other DNR personnel dragged several of the cages full of squirming otters down close to the water. And, of course, the media photographers with their usual, but unwarranted, privleges crowded around with whirring gizmos and other gear, blocking the view of those who had come to see the otters. It was worth thirty-three seconds on the evening news, I later noticed.

Braced, feet wide apart, I protected my Nikon from the high school boys on my left who had never seen a camera before and insisted on standing in front of it. They could be dealt with, though.

The real problem came from the five-year-old boy on my right who discovered that if you stamp your feet hard in the water, the water flies in all directions. I asked him to stop and pointed at the drops of water on my camera equipment. He ran behind his father's pant leg a few feet away.

The DNR speaker shouted something about how the school buses would be organized to pick up the masses after the event. Personally, I thought the DNR ought to unfurl one of its large river seines, pull it through the crowd, and drag the lot of us all the way to Tripoli. I loved the image, dwelt on it.

The moment was near, I thought. I couldn't be sure, since the media photographers were practically riding the cages as they were moved nearer the water. But, here and there, I got a glimpse of brown fur in the morning sun, and this fur seemed to be moving toward the quiet water of Sweet's Marsh.

I crouched behind my tripod and concentrated on focusing the Nikon. Wham! The five-year-old boy I sent away three minutes ago was back. He had discovered that if you smash the water with a stick, the water flies all over everything. I straightened up, tapped the short-bladed hunting knife that is a standard part of my outdoor kit, and said in a low baritone, "Swamp devil die young."

I wiped the water from my camera, while the kid disappeared toward his father. Ready now, here they come. One of the cages was opened, and three otters waddled toward the water. After that, it was bedlam.

The otters swam through the water, ran along the banks, and wrestled with one another in grass and sunshine. More otters were shown the water, and they knew what to do with it. The DNR man with the bullhorn shouted something about "rotating the crowd so everyone can see the otters." Nobody paid him any mind. Instead they slithered under the rope barricade and plunged toward the banks of Sweet's Marsh.

The program was just getting under way, but I packed my gear and walked to the car. I'll go back on some cold, rainy day in autumn, a few months from now. I judge it will take that long to get the ninth-grade boys back in their cages and for the yellow school buses to get loaded and back to Tripoli.

What can be concluded from this event? First, I'm glad the river otters are back in Iowa, and the people responsible for this are to be applauded without end. I truly mean that. I am amplified in spirit just knowing the otters are out there giving it a try.

Second, if I were a political candidate, I'd use my campaign contributions to corner the market on river otters and prodigiously announce the times and locations of their releases. Then, I'd get a sound system that works; I'd tell everybody how much I love river otters; I'd promise that we will never kill them, especially the babies. Furthermore, I'd promise that we will add more school bus drivers to supplement the existing twelve and that all books dealing with cooperative living will be burned at Sweet's Marsh as a testament to free speech. I'd be elected president of the galaxy.

Finally, in light of all the fun we had with the otter release at Sweet's Marsh, I'm rethinking some of my earlier recommendations about Iowa developing a tourist industry.

A Matter of Honor

Through cracks in the floorboard of an old Chevy truck, I watched a blur of gravel streaming by underneath my feet and thought about whatever twelve-year-old boys thought about in 1951. Baseball, maybe. Or, the still-distant possibility of girls. The dust blew in loose spirals behind us and lay finally upon the grass along the road, long after our passing.

My father drove, looking straight ahead, thinking of business, a Camel pinched between the first and second fingers of his left hand. I knew the look of him without turning. Blue cap, Oshkosh B'Gosh striped bib overalls, clean gray work shirt, wire-rimmed glasses.

At the end of his thin legs, high brown shoes worked the pedals of the truck that took us along the roads of summer. His right hand steered, and when a car or truck or tractor passed us going in the opposite direction, the first finger rose and dropped in the customary Iowa finger-wave.

I rode next to him, in the middle, a seating arrangment influenced by parental concern, since the passenger-side door had a tendency to swing open when we hit especially violent bumps. Larry, the hired man, dealt with the perils of the outside position and told me that chewing Wrigley's Spearmint gum while smoking tasted good.

I used to wonder if Larry might just disappear into the dust sometime, Spearmint gum and cigarette with him, the whirling child of a spring chuckhole wedded to a faulty door latch. But it never seemed to bother him. In those days, you took your risks and danced or fought at the Castle Club in Charles City on Saturday nights.

We were headed northeast out of Rockford toward a farm near Colwell. The Chevy, larger than a pickup and smaller than a grain truck, was loaded with chicken coops stacked high and roped down, cinched tight with the same slipknots I now use to fasten my canoe on car tops. The wire partitions for corraling feathered things that preferred not to be captured rattled between the coops and sideboards.

And wedged securely into the left-hand rear corner of the truck box was the Fairbanks & Morse portable scale. Though the scale was merely an intermediary device for converting poultry into money, the events surrounding it on this day would take the measure of something more than chickens.

We pulled into the farm yard of Ol' Lady Smith's place about eight in the morning. My father called most farm women "Ol' Lady." Age or looks had nothing to do with it. It was his preferred term, one that substituted for "Mrs." or "Miss" or anything else you could conjure up, and he meant no disrespect by the use of it. As for the last name, I am using "Smith" here because I cannot recall her name and wouldn't use it if I did remember.

Larry and I unloaded the scale and coops and catching equipment while my father talked amiably about weather and prices with the fortyish Ol' Lady Smith, sharpening his pencil with a jackknife. We had come to buy 750 leghorn broiler hens on this Wednesday.

I poured water into the sponge of the dust mask my father made me wear. His lungs suffered more from the dust of ten thousand chicken houses than from cigarettes, and he was determined that I would remain pure of breath for the tasks that awaited me in a larger world.

Wading into a large shed with hundreds of frightened, flying, running, screaming chickens is a torment I would reserve only for my enemies. But for eight summers that's what I did.

My father started me out in the back room of our produce house where we warehoused the chickens while waiting for semitrailer trucks that would take them onward to the cities. Sometimes there were thousands of birds back there, locked in what we called "batteries," which were large, rolling units of sixteen cages, five chickens to a cage.

That many chickens produces a fair amount of rather unpleasant output. Therefore, the least-favored task in the business was scraping and shoveling that nastiness into trucks for removal. On my first day of working for him, my father took me to the back room and provided me with a scraper, a shovel, and slender words that have fattened over the years: "Son, you'll always be able to say you started at the bottom." He smiled, touched me on the shoulder, and walked back to his office, while I contemplated the virtues of perdition relative to what I saw before me.

So I began there. After I had suffered long, and in silence, I was promoted to the truck where the air smelled of country mornings instead of manure, except for the chicken houses where the dust flew and the hard slash of ammonia instantly penetrated the most obscure places in your brain.

Larry and I set up the wire catch pen and drove part of the flock into it. Kneeling down, we grabbed the terrified and flapping hens by the legs, four in each hand, and carried them to the door where my father assiduously put them into the coops. When a dozen or so coops were filled, we went outside to help him weigh them while the Lady Smith watched closely.

Each coop had been weighed empty, with the tare carefully noted. Filled with chickens, the gross weight was observed and the net calculated.

My father checked the accuracy of the scale every week. And he went even further than that. I had learned how to round in my studies of arithmetic, but he had his own system. For any ounces over a given pound in gross weight, my father rounded up to the next whole pound, which meant the farmers consistently were receiving a large benefit in poundage.

I once asked him why he rounded as he did, for my textbooks instructed otherwise. His response was characteristically direct: "So nobody can ever accuse me of cheating them in the rounding, I always give the farmer the next higher pound, even if the weight is only an ounce over a given pound."

My father cherished his reputation for honest practice and strove to protect it, so I did not press him further, even though I knew his rounding procedures were arithmetically incorrect and financially draining. The trust in his methods was such that most farmers went on with other things while we collected their chickens and never questioned my father's numbers.

We were covered with dust, sweating in the June sun, and had loaded about five hundred of the hens when an event occurred that has stayed with me always. For some reason, Ol' Lady Smith accused my father of shorting her on the weights.

He was bent over the scale but straightened up slowly at her words, the Oshkosh B'Gosh bibs hanging from his bony shoulders. His face reddened in the kind of anger I only saw on certain occasions, such as that night when, caught in the frenzied grip of some glandular malfunction, I used my shortstop's arm to fire an apple through the screen door of a town official's home.

My father said nothing. He just looked at the Smith woman, looked at the sky, then looked at Larry and me. "I want you boys to take every goddamn chicken out of those coops, one at a time, very carefully, and put them all back in the chicken house." He closed his weight book with a slap, tucked it into the front pocket of his bibs, shoved his pencil in after it, and lit a Camel.

I was as angry as my father, for I had watched him lean against the currents of dishonesty time after time in his life and business. Larry didn't seem to care one way or the other. It was still four days to Saturday night, and whether we loaded chickens or unloaded them was of little concern to him.

So we put the chickens back into Ol' Lady Smith's chicken house, one by one, and carefully. At about chicken three hundred, she decided she had been wrong in her accusation and said so. My father refused to look at her. "Just keep unloading, boys," he instructed us.

The Smith lady began to apologize fervently. She pleaded with my father to take her broilers. He smoked, said nothing, and began to tie down the stacks of empty coops on the truck. We lifted the Fairbanks & Morse into its place, put the tailgates in their slots, and slid into the truck.

My father was silent all the way back to Rockford. His face was still red, and he worked his jaw back and forth in anger at the undeserved humiliation.

Then the phone calls began. Every night, Ol' Lady Smith would call our home and beg my father to come pick up her chickens. She knew our price was better than she could get anywhere else. You see, we had a contract with a large Milwaukee firm that specialized in supplying various ethnic groups in that city with certain types of food required for holiday occasions.

On Tuesdays, the Milwaukee folks would call and place their order with us: two thousand broiler hens about three to four pounds, six hundred capons, one hundred ducks, and so forth. Because of this custom work, my dad was able to pay higher than the market rate for poultry. He would call around the countryside, locate the needed stock, and make his deal over the phone. So the woman with the broiler hens regretted her spasm there in the dust of an Iowa farmyard, burdened more, I believe, by the threat of pecuniary loss than by any sense of true remorse.

This went on for about a week. Her broilers were growing too heavy for our needs, and she knew it. So did my father. Each evening, he spoke politely to her and said that he was not interested in doing business with her. Then one night, with no advance notice to any of us, he simply told her that we would be there first thing in the morning to get her chickens.

So we loaded Ol' Lady Smith's hens a second time. She chattered around, servile. My father was civil, but distant and cool. He weighed the chickens, wrote her a check out of the long book that said "Waller Produce Company" on the front, and sent Ol' Lady Smith's broiler hens to the ethnic groups of Milwaukee, covered as they were with both feathers and righteousness.

He bought her poultry for years after that and never once mentioned his fury at her accusation, though I knew it rested inside of him like a lump of hot chicken fat. His ultimate revenge was fair profit. He was both practical and principled. He could space the two when his honor was threatened and then close the gap when the time was right.

Matters of ethics and honor are difficult, can become confused and abstruse. You learn about such things not from books, but from example. You learn about them standing on your feet, in the sun outside of Ol' Lady Smith's chicken house, watching your father's face harden, his eyes turning to liquid hydrogen, his voice saying, "I want you boys to take every goddamn chicken out of those coops, one at a time, very carefully, and put them all back in the chicken house."

For honor is hard to come by. And pride that flows from honor is not false. Slowly, implicitly, you begin to understand that. You pick it up riding beside a thin and bony man in striped bib overalls, watching the Iowa roads run backward in time through the cracked floorboards of an aging truck, watching the dust blow in loose spirals behind you before coming to rest, once and finally, upon the summer grass, long after your passing.

Southern Flight

> Though boys throw stones at frogs in sport, the frogs do not die in sport, but in earnest.
>
> —BION

I am twenty birds back on the left side of the skein, looking over my shoulder at Malachi. He has taken many pellets in his eastern wing and cannot pull it high enough for a full stroke. My right leg is dragging as we hammer our way south in the late afternoon. Two pieces of shot are embedded there, and they will cause me great difficulty when we land.

We stayed too long in the north. All of us knew that. But the summer ran late and warm; we became fat, floated on amiable water, and delayed the leaving. Lobu had argued for days that it was time to go. But we whined or laughed at him and refused to rise when he urged us.

A cold night rain fell and turned to sleet by morning. We did not see four men take their places in long marsh grass when the sun was still far down the curve of Earth. At dawn, they began shooting while we were sleepy on the water.

Lobu sounded the lifting cry and was in the air at the first hint of camouflaged movement in the grass. I saw him begin to rise even before his warning slid across the pond. And I remember marveling at the great power of his young body, his wings taking him first along the water, then into a long curving roll as he fought for height and distance. I wondered if I had looked that splendid in my second year.

Others picked up the cry, and I knew this was more than Lobu's way of getting us moving. Amalo, one of the youngest geese, looked at me for a moment in panic and indecision. I signaled him instantly, reaffirming what he feared, and we began our takeoff, struggling desperately for speed, for another day, for another moment.

I called upon myself for the strength that once was there; I called upon myself for all that I had ever been. To my left, I could see a hunter swinging his dark barrel in a practiced, even way, following the wife of Jonaku through early light.

Coming off the water she exploded in a cloud of blood and feathers as the full load hit her. Jonaku trembled when he went over her floating body only two feet below him. The hunters were firing shell after shell from pump guns, and I could see pellets digging into the water ahead of me.

East we all were moving, perpendicular to the guns, straight into a curious mixture of freezing rain and rising sun. Birds were tumbling downward, some giving cries, others falling only in silence. The guns kept firing as I reached climbing speed. Malachi had drawn almost even with me, coming up on my left as we passed directly in front of the muzzles.

Rolling upward to the right. Apricot flame. A surge of it. Buffeting cone of mountain thunder. At the same moment I felt the impact on my leg, Malachi shuddered and began to fall, but caught himself and stayed low behind a stand of tall grass where the guns could not find him.

Sixty yards out. Almost safe. Coming around to follow Lobu, I could see a cumbrous man sloshing through the water, a spaniel beside him. He was shouting a wild cry of exultation and waving his gun above his head; I did not understand his words.

Birds were struggling, others lay still. Sori paddled in small, tight circles, flopping randomly, a piece of shot in her brain, while the dog swam toward her. Zachary, the old one, was injured, but tried one more time to follow us. As he flailed wildly near the edge of the pond, a man in camouflage shot him again, and he died there on northern water.

I banked into a strong wind from the western lands and fell into place. Other birds were doing the same. Water streamed from our feathers and flashed in the light of Mother sun, while Lobu took us southward.

There are two great rivers in the middle of this land. We are flying sixty miles east of the one that flows from the Montana highlands, three hundred miles north of the Missouri lakes. Ahead on the point, Lobu is pushing us hard. He is angry with us for lingering so long at the pond of morning, and we know he is right to be angry. Seven birds were killed by the hunters.

Light snow is falling. The color of the sky matches Lobu's mood. Our cadence has been steady for the last seven hours, and we listen to the Words. Heard they are, but not spoken. The sound unfolds from the meter of our wings. There is a slight unevenness in our stroking, and it is from this that the Words arise.

Like a great pulsing sigh they come, sweeping back along the lines in which we fly. "Alooooom" is the sound. "Alooooom – We Are One." It is our creed and our comfort.

The Words wash over me, and wondering about Malachi, I turn once more to look at him. I am startled to see blood coming from his left eye. I had not noticed the blood before, and I remember again that only his body saved me from the full load of shot. His good eye glitters with pain and desperation as he stares straight ahead, giving full energy to his flight.

Lobu is curving us around a tall structure with a round, dish-shaped plate at the top and over wires connected to it. We do not know the name of this thing, though we have seen many of them before.

Below, thin sheets of ice begin to form on shallow patches of water. The snow is falling with more intensity now, and each of us knows that we must keep moving. A blizzard would take many of us.

Ten yards across from me, in the western line, Shanta is

also watching Malachi. They are old lovers. She feels an enduring warmth for him and tries to send some of her strength over the empty sky between them.

When I had younger wings, the long southern flight was exhilarating. There were many places to come down and rest at evening. Now the water has disappeared. From this height, we can see traces of primitive contours where once the marshes could be found.

They are gone now. To other things they are gone. To houses and planted fields and roads. And there is little left for us.

Much of the remaining water is surrounded by guns, preserved only for the killing, not for the good. It is said the hunters fight with their money and their time to save the marshlands, and, though we try, we find it difficult to be grateful. We do not understand the killing; we can only fly before it.

The young ones ask about the killing. "Why?" they ask. We have no answers, for there seem to be none. Once there were reasons, the very old ones say, but those reasons disappeared long before the marshes died.

"But," the young ones press us, "if not for the meat, then why? And why have they taken the marshes if they want our flesh? It makes no sense!"

In those moments, we would turn to Zachary. He had lifted in terror from many ponds, had fought for the safety of altitude through a thousand magenta dawns with buckshot lacing the red face of Mother sun, had seen the waters smeared with blood and lifeless birds floating on silent mornings, had counted in his years the disappearance of the places for living. Finally he would speak, but only after the young ones could not be quieted with generalities and platitudes.

"I have no way of understanding the thoughts of humans. I can only repeat what has come down to me through the elders. The origins of what I will tell you are shrouded by the failure of memories and the embellishment of time. I know only that the words were given by one of many forms who rested on a long sandbar in summer firelight and spoke in a tongue that knew no boundaries. When the elders asked the same questions that you now ask about the ways of humans, they were cautioned to listen, to remember. And the traveler spoke thusly:

Ancient dreams, there are,
Unresolved.
And lingering impulses
From the days of rocks and fire,
Just after the great ice had gone.
A reluctance to come before
Themselves and ask,
'Who are we, and what is our place
Among all things?'

An avoidance, there is,
Of eternal questions,
Difficult and submerged.
Questions yielding not to
Force but only to
Subtle strands of
Intelligence and feelings
Woven full and pure
Into a cloth that
Catches the soft wind
Of enlightenment
Like a billowing,
Saffron-colored sail
Upon an endless river.

The answers are feared
So the questions are scuttled.
For the answers,
If they are firm

And truly given,
Would require change.
Those who profit now
Would profit less.

Enlightenment
Gives rise to
Kindness
And
Simplicity
And
Quietude.
Little profit
Can be found
In any of those.

And, like yourselves on a
Warm autumn day,
When it seems the
Croupier can be denied
Forever,
They are reluctant
To rise.

With that, he would swim away and pretend to busy himself at feeding along a shore where the wild rice yet grew. We will miss Zachary.

Word has traveled far, and we have heard about the condor and the falcon. And the little sparrows of the Florida swamps. We have seen the canvasbacks languishing and the streams turning dark with soil from the fields. The places for living are being taken or sullied with poison.

Behind me, I hear a small sound. I turn to look at Malachi and see his damaged wing flapping out of harmony with the good one. There is more blood coming from his injured eye. Fear screams from the other. He begins to fall away.

I start to follow him, but clearly he is gone. His bad wing

no longer is stroking, and I watch him drop toward a small grove of trees through a winter twilight. He crashes into branches and lies tangled there, hanging head down and still.

Southward we move, pounding through the snow with Lobu guiding us. The only sound I hear are the Words. From our wings they come, and sweeping back along the wind they find and comfort me.

Running into Perry

"Do you remember Perry Burgess? I'm his brother." I had just autographed a book for a man in a Marshalltown, Iowa, store and looked up.

Of course I remembered Perry. Instantly I could see him, forty years back along the cambers of my recollections. Dusty flatlands afternoon, high summer, Rockford, Iowa. Perry in work boots and cutoff jeans, shirtless, red bandanna tied around his head, good muscles. Slightly untamed and pretty close to what the counterculture folks looked like two decades later.

Perry, though, was permitted his quirks. Even in the hairy-chested culture of rural Iowa, where short pants on men were considered a telltale sign of unsteady masculinity. He was special, you see. He could handle the pounding heat of the kilns at the brick-and-tile plant in summer. As I recall, not many could. Maybe just him. He monopolized stamina. And that counted for something. Allowances could be made for Perry.

He carried his head at a slight angle; a bad eye might have caused that. Perry grinned a lot in those days, grinned at kids like me on the street in my old sneakers and jeans. I grinned back. I liked Perry. I liked his toughness and his style. I liked his good humor in the face of the brutal days he spent in the kilns. My mother has always remarked that my heroes were, well, a little different from those of other boys. I liked Kenny Govro, cat fisherman; Sammy Patterson, billiards player; and I liked Perry Burgess, kiln stacker.

When the annual softball game between the local merchants and the plant workers came around, it was understood Perry would be on the mound. "Perry 'The Dipsy-Doodler' Burgess." That's what he liked to be called in the weeks preceding the game. That's how the cardboard signs advertising the game listed him. That's what the local newspaper called him in announcements.

"Satch." He also liked to be called "Satch." I think that flowed from his respect for Satchel Paige, the great baseball pitcher. "Hey, Satch!" we'd yell at Perry Burgess. "Ready for the game?" He'd cock his head and grin.

Actually, he wasn't much of a pitcher. Given Perry's style, that was not the point. Under the lights of a country ball diamond, he pitched wildly, wheeled and dealed with seventeen different motions. Threw the ball behind his back, between his legs, the crowd roaring in approval. Old men in the stands whacked each other on the back and croaked, "That Perry Burgess, he sure is somethin' isn' he?"

On the mound, way out there in the dust with Satchel Paige riding his shoulder, Perry cocked his head and grinned at the applause, careened into his windup, and delivered another dipsy-doodler in the general direction of home plate. From kiln stacker to softball jester in three hours. Perry had range, that much was certain.

"Sure I remember Perry," I said out loud to his brother, Albert Burgess. "I'd love to see him again." "Well, he's right over there, sitting on a bench." Albert motioned, and across the floor of an Iowa shopping mall came Perry Burgess. Small, old, head cocked, grinning. I loomed over him, tall, taller than he'd ever been back there in the dusty days.

We shook hands. I grinned and told him about my feelings: "You were one of my heroes." Grabbing the book I had already signed, I wrote Perry's name in it, along with something about the esteem I held for him back down the years. I wanted to talk more, but there were books to be autographed, a stack of them. The holiday traffic was heavy.

Christmas music over the sound system. Perry and his brother drifted off, politely.

But I was warmed by seeing Perry again. Old feelings, good feelings. In my boyhood, Perry Burgess was one of the eagles and made those days better in ways still undefinable. Maybe it had to do with style, with flaunting convention and getting away with it. I don't know; it doesn't matter. The years run, but some of the old heroes are still out there, and I am comforted by that.

A few months later, in the summer, I wandered through the ruins of the tile plant. Weeds and trees have taken back the spaces where hard men worked the clay. There are spirits in that place. You'd have to be less than a quarter sentient not to feel them, to hear the shouts and footsteps, hear the freight cars rolling down the spur.

I came to the kilns. Three of them, with doors open, round and domed and thirty feet in diameter. Hornet nests in the cracks, dust blowing across the floors.

Sweating, August hot, I stood in one of the kilns for a moment, thinking of Perry. The image of an old man in a Marshalltown shopping mall was gone. That's not the way I see him. Nope. Not at all. This way: boots, cutoff jeans, no shirt, red bandanna around his head, good muscles. "Hey, Satch! Ready for the game?" Head slightly cocked, grinning, on the street outside of the beer joints, on the mound. That's how I remember Perry.

The ol' Dipsy-Doodler, out there under the lights, sliding into his windup, delivering. Darn right I remember him. He was important to me. Still is. It was good running into Perry.

The Trials of Hunter Rawlings

The University of Iowa recruits agile young men, many of them black and from distant cities, and lets them entertain us through the snap of November air and the hurtful cold of our winter nights. These young men, guided by the crisp athletic minds of people such as football coach Hayden Fry and basketball coach Tom Davis do what they're asked to do and do it well.

The touchdowns come, the stuff shots make the backboards tremble, the bowls and the tournaments send out invitations, and Iowans are content. In a state that suffers from geographical anonymity, along with a curious and self-imposed sense of cultural inferiority, apparently many Iowans believe that successful college athletic teams provide them with legitimate national bragging rights, of sorts.

Comes now into our midst one Hunter Rawlings III, princely of both name and spirit. After a somewhat jumbled effort at finding a decent president for the University of Iowa, the state's Board of Regents hired Rawlings and gave him the explicit charge of making the university a place of academic excellence. Rawlings, it seems, has taken that directive seriously. A little too seriously, for some.

Hunter Rawlings III, you see, is fed up with the shallow academic performance of many university athletes and the dishonesty that seems to accompany top-drawer collegiate athletic enterprises. He believes that athletes ought to learn something aside from how to execute a four-corner offense, late in the game, early in their lives. So as spring came to the flatlands, the April light thin and yellow and warming, Rawlings announced his recommendations:

–Lobby the National Collegiate Athletic Association to ban freshman from playing for or practicing with athletic teams.
–If the NCAA does not adopt such a ban within three years, the University of Iowa should do it unilaterally.
–College sports seasons should be shortened.
–The practice of housing athletes together in University of Iowa dormitories should be ended.
–Athletes who are convicted of crimes should be banned from their teams.
–Universities should be required to make public the graduation rates of their athletes, with the rates broken down by the athletes' race and sport.

The *Exxon Valdez* oil spill and the annual meeting of the Iowa Legislature had to fight for newspaper space in competition with the debate over Rawlings's proposals. Considerably less uproar would have been generated if Rawlings had urged Iowans to cut back on the consumption of red meat in the interest of good health or had come out in favor of rural school consolidation.

The opposition to his plan has been emotional, intense, self-serving, and poorly argued. But he's taken heat. God how he's taken heat. Most of the criticism surrounds his proposal to eliminate freshman eligibility and practice.

The *Des Moines Register*'s April 12 headline screamed in six columns: "Fry 'mad as hell,' hints he'd quit." "Iowans united in opposition to benching freshman athletes" was the April 16 headline following the *Register*'s Iowa Poll.

The poll, for which the *Register* claims accuracy to within 4.8 percentage points, indicated that 74 percent of Iowans object to the restrictions on freshman play and practice. It is worth noting that only 13 percent of those who claim to be University of Iowa athletic fans ever attended classes there. In a separate poll the following day, just 34 percent of Iowans approved of the way Hunter Rawlings is handling his job at the university, judging him, one supposes, on the single criterion of athletic management.

Iowa Governor Terry Branstad, who should have known better than to involve himself in this quarrel, argued against Rawlings's position: "We must also recognize athletics is part of the extracurricular activities in colleges and at larger universities it is very important and significant. It is also a source of entertainment for many people who never went to college themselves."

It gets worse. The letters-to-the-editor column in the *Register* has been an embarrassment to a state that continually toots about its scores on national achievement tests, such as the ACT and SAT. (Iowans never seem to realize that, in addition to possessing a rather decent educational system, one reason we look so fine on such tests is that we have a low proportion of people in the disadvantaged groups from which many good athletes come.)

One writer ultimately opposed to Rawlings's position stated: "The suggestions of the University of Iowa is commendable." Another: "If they're good enough to enroll at U of I, then let 'em play ball!" Another: "Why don't we get rid of Hunter and keep our sports program?" Another: "Do we want to be recognized as another Northwestern?" That last one is especially perverse. Given Northwestern's fine academic reputation, I suspect that Rawlings would answer "Yes, absolutely!" to the question posed.

Then there was Jim Walden, football coach at Iowa State University and would-be social philospher, who was quoted as saying: "I'm opposed to idle time. To say they should not be allowed to practice is against the American way. Idleness is the devil's workshop. When do you see most athletes get in trouble? It's not during the season."

That's one to paste on your sunglasses. If I were Gordon Eaton, president of Iowa State, I'd ask for Walden's resignation on the grounds of (1) misunderstanding both time and patriotism, (2) getting the proverb wrong, and (3) harmful blither and terminal cliches.

In Tama, Iowa, with cigarette smoke swirling and Hawkeye banners flying at the Eagles lodge, the local I-Club gave Hayden Fry standing ovations during his appearance there shortly after Rawlings's announcement. No discussion, it seems, was held concerning recent developments in the Ethiopian hunger crisis.

Then fifteen influential members of the mother I-Club met, denounced Rawlings, and even had the temerity to demand that he apologize to Iowans and University of Iowa coaches for insulting "their intellectual efforts and the emphasis placed on college athletics."

On the other hand, the University of Iowa faculty senate supports Rawlings. So do the *Register,* the Iowa Board of Regents, and at least fifty other Iowans, including me, except I believe his plan should be even more draconian.

Rawlings's proposals were a semi-gut-level response to some rather nasty revelations that emerged during the trial of sports agents Norby Walters and Lloyd Bloom, which included testimony from two former Iowa football players, Devon Mitchell and Ronnie Harmon.

The legal strategies got a little vague, but generally the prosecution's idea was to prove that Walters and Bloom aided various athletes in defrauding universities by providing the players with monies while they were still on scholarship ($54,000 to Harmon). The defense attempted to counter these allegations by trying to show that the universities were of such low mind and spirit that they, themselves, were acting in a fraudulent manner by allowing players on the field who, at best, were students only in the most nominal sense.

Mitchell and Harmon, testifying under immunity-from-prosecution agreements, said they attended the University of Iowa to play football and not much else. As part of the testimony, the two player's transcripts were made public, and these transcripts bore out what Mitchell and Harmon had said about their academic aspirations. For example, Mitchell's course selections in the first semester of his 1981 freshman year included billiards, bowling, karate, ancient athletics, football, coaching basketball, a vocational education course, and two remedial courses in writing and reading.

He rose to the challenge and received a 2.22 grade-point average, on a four-point scale, for his efforts. During his last semester at Iowa, in 1986, Mitchell enrolled for five courses, withdrew from four, and received an incomplete in "First Aid and CPR." In between, his academic record is what generous institutional officials like to call "spotty."

Harmon's academic record was only slightly better than his performance in the 1986 Rose Bowl, where he fumbled four times. Much derisive snorting has occurred, in particular, over his grade of D in a watercolor painting course. As someone with rather serious interests in the visual arts, I particularly take issue with that complaint, since watercolor painting is a fairly demanding medium.

Though Walters and Bloom were found guilty of defrauding the University of Michigan and Purdue University, they were judged not guilty of fraud in the Michigan State and Iowa instances. Lawyers for Walters and Bloom had argued that questionable conduct by the latter two universities made it impossible for them to be defrauded.

One juror, after reviewing the transcripts of Harmon and Mitchell, said: "I thought it was a travesty of higher education. It is appalling." Apparently she was not moved by the claims of Iowa assistant athletic director Fred Mims that the two players were, indeed, eligible at all times and were progressing toward degrees.

While all of this was emerging, two Iowa State University athletes attempted a holdup at an Ames Burger King. Both men received bullet wounds from the guns of policeman as a result of whatever occurred. One of them, Levin White, pleaded guilty to first-degree robbery. The other, Sam Mack, was acquitted on the grounds that he was coerced into the mess by White.

Then *Time* magazine, in its April 3, 1989, edition, reported that basketball player Lafester Rhodes left Iowa State with minimal reading and writing skills after playing there from 1984 to 1988. According to the former Topeka Sizzlers coach, Art Ross, Rhodes had considerable difficulty in reading and filling out his application form for the team. And there was the matter of three University of Iowa basketball players being treated for substance abuse in the summer of 1988.

Gazing around himself at the smoke and carnage, Hunter Rawlings said, "Enough!" Like Clint Eastwood in one of the old spaghetti westerns, Rawlings rode in, surveyed the situation, and decided the town was worth saving. The hitch is that the town may not want to be saved.

What's going on here? First of all, the admissions by Mitchell and Harmon that their reasons for attending college had little to do with intellectual growth should not astonish anyone who has the least familiarity with big-time college athletics. There are, of course, athletes who do distinguish themselves academically.

For the most part, however, that is not the case. Thirty hours of practice time per week along with the psychological milieu in which such athletes exist make high achievement extremely difficult. And anyone who believes in the student-athlete concept as it relates to the searing pressure of big-time sports is either dumb or not paying attention or has suffered the kind of lobotomy that results from undue attention to the trivial and transitory.

Oh, athletic departments are fond of trotting out figures to show that athletes have higher graduation rates than non-athletes. That's not very convincing, to me at least. I want to know in what fields of study the athletes have graduated, what courses they took, who taught the courses, what grades they received, and something about the overall rigor of the classes. In general, athletics do not mix well with curriculums that demand long hours of laboratory work, contemplation, the pursuit of difficult mathematical proofs, extensive reading lists, and at least six hours of study per day.

But there's something more fundamental at work here. It has to do with immaturity and major flaws in the entire American educational system and, hence, our society. I still remember the words of a humanities professor from Florida who published an essay years ago. In that piece is a sentence that fairly rings with an essential and basic truth. It went something like this: "Anyone who graduates from college and five years later cares whether or not the athletic teams from that college win should consider his or her education a failure."

I happen to agree, completely, with that statement. Whether or not the University of Northern Iowa or Indiana University, both of which have been kind enough to grant me degrees, wins or loses in athletics means nothing to me. Period. It means nothing to me because it means nothing in general.

But it's important to many people. And therein lies a tragedy of our lives and the failure of education in this country. Consider it. Why did Hunter Rawlings receive the kind of abuse that he did and where did it come from?

Well, it didn't emanate from the students at the University of Iowa. And it didn't come from the faculty. It came from adults who should know better.

The scolding that Rawlings has endured gushes mostly from so-called grownups outside the university who know very little about how the academic world really functions or, at least, is supposed to function. Moreover, in spite of protestations to the contrary about the importance of academics, these critics really don't care how the unviversity carries out its business as long as it provides winning athletic teams and issues degrees and bowl tickets to their children.

What they're really whining about is the possible loss of personal entertainment and misplaced pride flowing from the skills of young men who actually think these fans care about them as human beings. Former athletes at our universities who did not enter the professional ranks are the first to admit this. They are shocked at the sudden loss of adulation that accompanies the termination of their playing careers. If you're not on the court, you're not on television, and, therefore, you are no longer in our hearts. They are singers with one hit song who fade into that curious oblivion reserved for those who achieve modest athletic prominence.

And the entertainment aspect spills beyond the boundaries of the games themselves. The tailgate parties, the athletic fundraising dinners, the golfing outings, the restaurant talk—they're all part of it. They form an interlocked social and economic subsystem that has little to do with the intellects and lives of the people who play the games. As one Iowa fan put it: "I could walk up to a stranger that had a Hawk cap or jacket on and start an enthusiastic conversation about 'our Hawks.' " So there is that and the fact that football Saturdays in Iowa City bring approximately $1 million per game into town.

Iowa stores are full of athletic memorabilia. Caps, jackets, sweatshirts, jogging suits, coffee cups, and dozens of other items. University of Iowa trinkets are most favored, followed by those linked with Iowa State and the University of Northern Iowa. And, believe it, there is big money involved here.

In the city where I live, a man painted the mascot

emblems of the three state universities on his garage doors. He admitted a bias toward the University of Iowa, and, therefore, made Herky the Hawk a little larger than the University of Northern Iowa panther and the Iowa State cyclone or bird or whatever it is. The newspaper that reported this story treated the man's endeavors as cute. I consider that sort of personal attention devoted to college athletic teams prima facie evidence of a foolish and wasted life.

Then, of course, there's television. And the sports magazines and the daily sports sections of major newspapers. And radio. And the sports books of Vegas. It all interlocks and becomes mutually self-supporting. The players play, but the big guys, the money folks, know what's really going on, and it has nothing, absolutely nothing, to do with learning or concern for the personal welfare of young athletes in the long run.

The foundation upon which this entire superstructure rests is the fan. Without the fan, the person who supposedly watches television advertisements during timeouts, makes donations to athletic funds, and buys tickets to the games, the whole business collapses. What's sad and a little frightening here is that people's lives apparently are so empty of belief in themselves and the ability to provide their own emotional satisfaction that they must rely on the prowess of young men, boys really, who run and jump and block and tackle and pass and punt while pretending to be serious students.

This probably sounds a little superior. I hope not, for I don't feel superior. Hell, I'm pretty much in favor of anything that is not socially destructive or environmentally damaging and prevents people from injuring themselves or others in the muddle of some existential funk.

What we're talking about, though, is something less than candor, something this side of complete honesty, a kind of lie-with-a-wink attitude that is doing disservice to our universities, to our players, and, most of all, to ourselves. We know the current state of college athletics is neither good nor true to the academic ideal, and yet we persist in lying to ourselves and each other for the sake of some shallow participation as spectators and worshipers of transitory heros. We are watchers at the pond, not swimmers.

That's where part of the tragedy rests, for in the interest of our private, selfish enjoyment we also mislead the swimmers about their importance to us and the value of their product. As one old western movie gunfighter said to another when asked what he currently was doing, "Me? I jus' hang around and keep tellin' lies to children."

A lot of former athletes, and current fans, are doing exactly that. So, for our own selfishness, to quiet the voice of our own inadequacies, we lie—to the players, to each other, to ourselves, and, perhaps most damaging, to the very young who hear the applause given by their parents to athletes and strive to receive this applause at all costs, including the cost of their own development as complete human beings.

And that's where Hunter Rawlings got in trouble. You see, he was thinking about the welfare of young athletes and the progress of his university. What he really didn't consider, perhaps, was the larger social and economic structure that supports the nonsense, the lies, the duping of our young.

He also made another mistake, a managerial one. In his haste to take action, to appear decisive, he neglected to meet with his coaches and athletic directors, and maybe the heads of the booster (lord, how I hate that word!) clubs ahead of time. There was too much shock in the way he made the announcement. People do not like nasty surprises, and athletic coaches are no exception to this.

I can understand Hayden Fry's histrionics, though his periodic threats to quit if his wants are not assuaged get unbelievably tiresome. Fry is not the only person who fashioned the world in which he operates. Like the rest of the big-time coaches, he's on a runaway train, and all he can think about is how to hang on—not how to stop it, even if he wanted to. He's a captive of a sick and failing system. So, he was surprised, saw Rawlings's proposals as a threat to his world, and reacted.

Still, even if he made some tactical managerial errors, I admire Hunter Rawlings for his courage, his plain and unabashed guts. It appears he acted almost instinctively from a strong and fundamentally correct set of values concerning the real purpose of a university and the humane treatment of young men who have been sorely misled about what is right, about what really matters in the long run.

You don't get that kind of wonderful, lofty, and righteous passion out of management textbooks, you don't get it from watching the antics of Donald Trump, and you don't get it from watching college sports as a spectator. As one supporter of Rawlings wrote in a letter to the *Register:* "If Hunter Rawlings III isn't careful, he'll be ranked with James B. Conant of Harvard and Robert Hutchins of the University of Chicago as one of the great educators of this century."

Winding its way through the mess at Iowa, and big-time college athletics in general, is the matter of decision making. Bad academic decisions. Rising to his own defense, and rolling out a little of his Texas-boy language at the same time, Hayden Fry said: "But what is Iowa guilty of? Not a cotton-picking thing. Our people are entitled to enroll in a program that the university offers." And: "The supposedly rinky-dink courses are set up by academicians, not the athletic department. At no time in my coaching history has the coaching staff had anything to do with the curriculum."

All right, let's grant Fry a minor point on that issue. University curriculum committees—faculty—approve curriculums and individual courses. Ultimately, the Iowa Board of Regents grants its approval.

Fry likes to characterize the University of Iowa as a great

university. It is not a great university yet, though it might become one. In addition to more esoteric measures of greatness, no front-rank insitution would allow a course in Advanced Slow Pitch Softball on the books.

I question the value of even a beginning course in that subject, but I'll bow to the need for students to learn something about recreation and how their bodies function along with the thin, left-brained intellectualism that dominates college instruction. Personally, I learned to play softball by batting against big farmers who could windmill a softball pitch across the plains of Iowa at over a hundred miles an hour on dusty Sunday afternoons. But that was another time, I suppose.

Thus, the faculty is to blame for allowing a course in the higher intricacies of slow pitch softball and similar bits of marshmallow in the catalog. The curriculum committee could have said no, and it should have. But Fry is being more than a little disingenuous by arguing that athletic advisors simply chose from what was available.

Devon Mitchell's courses during his first and subsequent semesters can only be characterized as a bastardization of everything that going to college means. Those advising Mitchell could have selected a more typical schedule for his first semester, including a basic college mathematics course, something in the humanities and natural sciences, the study of history, and maybe a good, solid piece of work in philosophy.

That's naive, right? Of course it is. Obviously, the athletic department's academic advisors believed that Mitchell could not handle such a standard course load and would have been ineligible. After all, he needed remedial work in reading and writing. The point is, of course, that while living within the rules of the university, selecting courses listed in the schedule, Mitchell's academic advisors carried out a cynical mockery of all that higher education is supposed to mean.

And why the mockery? So Mitchell could be eligible.

And why should Mitchell be eligible? So the Hawks could use his talents to win games and satisfy the screaming and immature fans who, quite frankly, could care less about Mitchell's course of study and whether he was being prepared for a life beyond football.

Hunter Rawlings knows all of this. What he may not completely grasp is that he is tangled in the clash of two distinct cultures. On the one hand, there are those so bereft of individual skills and personal resources that they must find solace in the performance of young men for whom shaving is a new experience.

On the other side are those who believe in the life of the mind and the spirit, who believe in rich self-fulfillment through knowledge and the arts, including the physical arts of recreation. Rawlings belongs to the latter group. So do I. If that makes us elitists, so be it, though I don't think it does. I think it labels us as sane.

College athletics is a frenzied animal that slowly and inexorably is devouring itself. I see no lasting answers to be found in tinkering with the present system.

Perhaps, as some suggest, a ban on freshman eligibility will help. But I rode a pretty fair long-range jump shot out of high school to a scholarship at the University of Iowa thirty years ago and saw most of the same problems that we have today, even when freshmen were not allowed to join the varsity and athletes were not housed in their own dormitories. In those days, Forest Evashevski, a man to be feared far more than Hayden Fry, stalked the Iowa fieldhouse like a lion, and the academic gazelles ran before him.

Maybe paying coaches salaries comparable to regular faculty and giving them tenure is part of the answer. If, however, you're making $500,000 from a combination of salary, revenue from summer camps, television shows, and the like, it's going to be pretty difficult to support that proposal.

Check with Rick Pitino about that. He recently signed a

seven-year contract to coach basketball at the University of Kentucky that will provide him with an estimated income of $800,000–$900,000 per year. So ask him, "Rick, don't you think we ought to cut back on the importance of athletics just a little?"

Other suggestions offered include the reduction of practice time, having games only on weekends, requiring coaches to snitch on other coaches when violations of standards are observed, and stiffening entrance requirements for athletes.

If all of these are adopted, college athletics likely will be reduced to just a cut above club sports, which is about where I think it ought to be. For example, the Iowa Conference still adheres to most of the original intents of collegiate sports, and I applaud them for it.

To the extent that athletic coaches have a say in the matter, however, none of this will be done; the disincentives are too great. Though some enlightened coaches sick of fans and boosters and arbitrary dismissals based on win-loss records might be ready to support a subset of the current proposals.

The very worst of the recommendations floating around involves treating the players as professionals and simply paying them for their services. I doubt if this is economically feasible, particularly if the level of competition is reduced by other rules.

In addition, and much more important, such a system is unthinkable in light of what universities proclaim to be their central mission—the pursuit of truth, the education of students, the betterment of our world. Those who favor treating college athletes as professionals do not understand the unholiness of a marriage between athletics as a business and the academic enterprise.

About the only solution I can see is for the university presidents to agree, in a headlong denial of what they currently perceive to be self-interest, that the entire situation is out of hand, athletic revenues and false prestige notwithstanding, and agree to substantial reductions in the level of competition. If we must have competitive sports for entertainment, as our governor believes, the reduction in the level of collegiate competition should be accompanied by the development of a farm system in all major sports similar to that used by baseball (although baseball, unfortunately, also has come to view universities as a cost-free minor league).

If fans are willing to support professional athletics in various classes, then a system of major and minor leagues in all popular sports will survive. If such support is not forthcoming, then it will prove that the various implicit subsidies provided by universities and those who support them through taxes or other means are all that really keeps high-powered collegiate athletics alive. That and the rosy illusion that what we are seeing on the field is a group of young folks who have been reading Kant all morning just before arriving at the stadium. That illusion somehow is part of the current nonsense.

After all, taxpayers subsidize college athletics in many subtle ways, such as university parking lots, dormitory construction, the use of police and state troopers for crowd control, highway maintenance, insurance, and so forth. I never, for a moment, have believed that athletic departments are entitled to all the revenues they profess to generate.

I suspect a first-class audit would disclose indirect costs being incurred all over the place that are not charged to athletic functions. Society pays a substantial portion of the freight, and the so-called profits derived from major sports likely are nonexistent or at least are less than usually proclaimed.

So, we can set up professional leagues with no organizational relationships to the schools, rent the existing university facilities to these teams at a price covering all costs, pay the coaches and players what the market says they're worth, and even toss in the old black and gold or purple and gold uniforms until the teams can buy their own. They even can keep the team logos and nicknames, for all I care.

In other words, we'll let the market decide the worth of the enterprise. All right-thinking conservatives, and true Americans in general, certainly will be in favor of this approach.

Moreover, there are reasonable, intelligent people who simply enjoy watching competitive athletics the way others of us entertain ourselves by watching films or reading or playing the guitar. A market-based plan works for these folks as well, since they can decide whether or not to spend their recreational time and dollars on spectator sports formerly sponsored by universities.

For boosters, the de-academizing of athletics results in a perfect world. They can kick in all the money and cars they want to without the sneaky, annoying intrusions of the NCAA. And no more Proposition 42 worries here. Those who want to become professional athletes can forget about astronomy, concentrate on blocking, and possibly earn at least the minimum wage in the process.

None of what I propose will be any more damaging to the academic spirit than, choking as I say it, renting out the UNI-Dome for car-crunching by a giant, internal combustion vehicle called "Bigfoot." And if there is duplication in athletic events and facilities, a subject seemingly not addressed in the recent study of duplication in the universities of this state, we'll let the market sort that out, too.

As for disadvantaged young people (read that "athletes") losing the opportunity to attend college, I, for one, am willing to pay more taxes to make this happen, as long as their recruitment and admission is based on intellectual and artistic skills rather than well-developed abilities in what are essentially recreational pastimes that have been taken to ludicrous heights.

In the end, then, Rawlings is correct, though his approach may have been a little crude. He knows, I know, and anybody who has given ten minutes of serious thought to the situation knows that we have a savage burlesque on our hands. We have a warping of all that universities are supposed to stand for, and should stand for, and this warpage is being supported by those who have no sense of the academic ideal and could care less about it if they did.

Yet, the *Register* recently published a series of letters on the University of Iowa situation with a covering headline that read: "The last word on U of I college athletics vs. academics." I sincerely hope the editors don't really mean the debate over the proper role of collegiate athletics is, in their minds, closed.

The problem has not gone away. The knee ligaments are still tearing, the deceit continues. The chicanery goes on, and, to be fair, it's probably more severe at some other universities than it is at the University of Iowa, though we should not decrease the intensity of our debate just because our universities may sin less.

Recently, a writer from *Sports Illustrated* asked me what I thought would happen if it really came down to a firefight between Rawlings and the coaches/fans/politicans faction. Could Rawlings survive? I hesitated for a moment, and I didn't like the fact that I was hesitating. But I recovered and told him that the Iowa Board of Regents historically has shown courage in supporting academic principles, standing firm in the face of assaults on those principles, and that I believe they would stand firm in this matter as well, supporting and encouraging Rawlings in his laudable efforts.

Hunter Rawlings has drawn a line in the sand. Those of us who still care about education and truth and the removal of a dangerous and debilitating hypocrisy from our lives should step over it with him. And if the image and pride of Iowa, as a state, is dependent upon the athletic performance of young men who are not old enough to understand what's really going on, then we are less of a people than I once thought we were.

. . . .

This essay was written in the spring of 1989. On January 9, 1990, two days before the book manuscript was delivered to the publisher, the NCAA approved a number of reforms designed to reduce the pressure on athletes. The reforms were viewed as a victory for the NCAA's Presidents Commission, a forty-four-member advisory panel. One motivating force for the changes was a survey disclosing that college athletes, particularly those playing football and basketball, spent more time on sports than on academics.

University athletic directors and coaches had opposed the reforms and attempted to block passage of them through parliamentary maneuvering and other tactics. Some athletic directors commented that the university presidents were usurping the athletic directors' roles. The directors were also concerned that at least one of the reforms, a reduction in the number of basketball games each season, will result in financial loss for their programs, with estimates ranging from $250,000 to $500,000 per school. Vanderbilt Athletic Director Roy Kramer said: "That's a lot of money. Idealism reigned today, but realism will set back in pretty soon."

The delegates to the convention also approved, overwhelmingly, to adopt rules requiring Division I and Division II members to issue annual reports showing a five-year average graduation rate of athletes by sport, by sex, and by race. Other changes approved dealt with reducing the length of spring football practice and delaying conditioning, practice, and competition in basketball by about two weeks. "Our athletes have sent us a clear message that they need time to be students," said Lattie Coor, president of Arizona State University. "We are placing just too many demands on our student-athletes."

On the same day the reforms were announced, two University of Iowa basketball players were declared academically ineligible, a third was suspended indefinitely after being charged with an alcohol-related violation, and Lauro Cavazos, education secretary, declared American schoolchildren are "dreadfully inadequate" in reading and writing, as he released the results of two nationwide studies.

The Lion of Winter

Felis concolor, middle-brown in the thin light of a winter afternoon, comes out of the scrub thirty feet ahead of me, three hundred yards from the Pacific. She crosses the old Park Service road in easy strides and, without hesitating, takes her one hundred pounds into a soft curving leap over a patch of low brush on the other side, like a house cat arching into a cardboard box.

Instinctively then, I am into a crouch and turning to the woman behind me. "Did you see the lion?" I say quietly. "What?" she answers, confused. "The mountain lion, the cougar, did you see it?"

For a moment she doesn't believe me. I can tell. Another of my little stories, she thinks; the outdoor man teasing the indoor woman again. From my shoulder comes the knapsack, and I dig frantically within it for a camera. "A what? Where?" the woman asks again, earnestly. I tell her and begin to move slowly up the narrow and abandoned road, toward the place where the cat has gone into the brush.

Only two miles behind, the van rests on a highway's edge. Back there is air conditioning and speed, concrete and the road to cities. Here, the technological ground is different, tilted a bit in favor of the lion. And, in some curious way, I relish that. She is at home, and I am the stranger. A kind of interspecies democracy has taken hold, and my place in the food chain seems less secure than it did a few minutes ago.

Staring hard, my eyes watering from the energy of focus, I reach the brush and look into it. Nothing. Further up the road in quiet steps, I stop and look long into the grass and brambles. Nothing.

Disappointed and turning toward the woman, I catch the breath of her whisper on the wind of late afternoon: "It's here. It's right here." She looks back into the tangle, then at me, partly confused, partly afraid.

Carefully, I go back along the road, my boots silent on old dirt, until I stand beside the woman and look where she is looking. And there is the face, a young one but old enough to be on her own, looking back at me from ten feet away—the eyes yellow-green, white fur around the mouth and chin, whiskers silver-gray in the mottled light, ears pointing up.

For a moment, just a moment, the eyes of order Carnivora and order Primates come together. I look at her. She stares back, unblinking. Then, perhaps catching a faint and lingering smell of the spear, she is gone, not even as a shadow, but rather like the dream of one. No branch flickering, no crackling of brush, no sound at all.

In the ways only cats are given, she just swings her head, moves off, and leaves us standing there along a road, by a river, near the sea. The one frame of film I remember to shoot as she goes eventually develops into a brown, out-of-focus blur. I will throw it in the discard box. The memory of such things is always better than a photograph, anyhow.

The woman and I move on toward the sea, talking of lions and yellow-green eyes and the wondrous good fortune of seeing the cat. Just the night before we had been driving along a mountain road, headlights sweeping thick forest on the curves, and I had said, "There are only a few things I need to do yet in my life; one of them is to see a mountain lion in the wild." So we talk about that and other matters of chance.

As we walk toward the beach, I am silent about the fact that big cats have been known to follow humans, if only out of some passing curiosity. Now and then, however, I glance backward along the path and into the trees. Truly, though, we have little to fear. The number of attacks on humans by mountain lions statistically is low. But, as one biologist has pointed out, mountain lions can't count. Later, I tell an official from the Mountain Lion Coalition about our meeting with the cat, and she says, "Do you realize how special that is?" I do. The probability of such an encounter is incredibly small. The big cats, nocturnal and secretive, are twilight figures even to those who seek to study them.

Except for thirty or so Florida panthers, and their survival is tenuous, the eastern lands are pretty much empty of lions. Killed as vermin or game or their habitat destroyed, they have gone. Though some believe that the cougars or pumas or mountain lions or catamounts, all of them the same animal, are moving back into remote areas of New England, northern Minnesota, and Michigan as forests regenerate and the deer population increases.

Aside from the perverse human tendency to destroy anything that offers the least bit of threat, the loss of range is the true vandal of the cougar's world. They are the ultimate individualists, loners except at mating time, and the consummate travelers, requiring a space of forty to two hundred square miles for their hunting.

Their range, particularly in the Far West, unceasingly falls to the saw and the highway and the condominium. California alone has lost 7.7 million acres of lion habitat since the 1800s, 4.5 million of those acres since 1945.

Moreover, as with all cats, the lions are uncooperative, even when humans are trying to help them. Estimates of the lion population are disputed vigorously among various groups interested in the cougar's preservation. The truth is that nobody knows for sure how well or poorly the lions are faring, and the big cats aren't talking.

Still, I had that moment. And I claim as much for it as any of the things I have seen. I have looked into the eyes of a starlight traveler whose lands recede steadily now. So, like the wild spaces themselves, I also grow less in contemplating a world too small and too selfish and too beset upon the trivial and transitory for the allowance of freedom, freedom that is colored middle-brown in the light of a winter day and carefully must keep to ever-diminishing cover.

I sigh within myself at the losses we sustain, the cat and I, for each of us understands in our own fashion that range, free range, is the way to the center of things. To take that from a traveler is to take all—from the traveler, from ourselves. And freedom thus becomes not even like a shadow, but rather like the dream of one. Like a dream I once had out along the edge of the great ice, a long time ago, before wisdom came and, along with other childish things, I put the spear aside.

Frontiers, Part I

> "How many of you know what's important?" Up went all the hands. "Very good," said Stuart, cocking one leg across the other and shoving his hands in the pockets of his jacket. "Henry Rackmeyer, you tell us what is important." "A shaft of sunlight at the end of a dark afternoon, a note in music, and the way the back of a baby's neck smells if its mother keeps it tidy," answered Henry. "Correct," said Stuart. "Those are the important things. . . ."
>
> —E. B. WHITE, *Stuart Little*

The original idea, where we started out, was to escape raw necessity and thereby leave time for music and the dance and poetry and, in general, the expansion of our creative selves to the fullest. Somewhere along the way, we got lost. The process itself became the goal, and now it seems almost naive, maybe quaint, to speak of leisure and the search for personal fulfillment.

We're too busy for that. Too busy doing what? That's not clear anymore, particularly for those some distance above the poverty line. Earning money is the easy response, I guess. For what reason? Well, obviously, so things can be purchased. What things? Education. Okay, that's reasonable, on the surface at least. Why education? To get a good job. Why would you want that? To earn money. So, having arrived at the beginning again, I ask, "Why more money?" To buy things. What else besides education? A better house. What's better? More space? More kitchen cupboards and a fireplace and shag carpet and a great big sofa and a great big high-definition television set when it comes along? Yeah, that's the idea.

What else? Dumb question. Lots of stuff. The stores are full of it. The catalogs in my mailbox are crammed with things having little real function other than to be bought. A quick run through "The Sharper Image" catalog is an exercise in disbelief, for me at least. "For crying out loud," I ask, "Do we really need all of this junk?"

Maybe that's why bigger houses are required—to have a place for the stuff we bought with our educations. Ask the shoppers with their noses plastered against the front doors of Target or Wal-Mart on the day after Thanksgiving, waiting for the store to open; they'll tell you. Stuff. Lots of it. Good Stuff, presents. Things that flash and things that go whirr and $125 sneakers for the kids who simply must have them, because everyone else apparently must have them.

And, of course, something for Dad. How about a video tape of great bloopers in sports? Or an all-terrain vehicle? Or that television set with a big screen so he can watch all the games in style? That's the marketer's image of the American male: shallow, uncontemplative, a connoisseur of pass rushes and easy chairs and internal combustion engines. For love do we carry on so? Nonsense. Love has nothing to do with $125 sneakers and sports bloopers. In fact, the mindless pursuit of trinkets works directly against romance and love, for those require time and appreciation of intangibles.

It's starting to get a little frightening. You can find people out there earning $100,000 a year with nothing in the bank, a suffocating mortgage, and $20,000 in short-term debt on top of it, a legacy of pulling the plastic out too many times. Still, it comes at us, unrelentingly, the advertising does, along with the peer-group pressures and the general celebration of high-intensity consumption.

The legitimacy of America is now defined not in terms of enlightenment or concern for those less fortunate or the nurturing of democracy, but rather in terms of economic growth. And growth, as we have defined it, is dependent upon the constant stimulation of creatures who used to think of themselves as citizens. The marketers know better. We are consumers—and don't you forget it!—furry little creatures requiring constant stimulation and phony innovation lest we neglect our proper role, which is not to live, but to buy. In the parlance of contemporary hucksterism, we are "targets" for "units."

And why should we buy? Because more is better and less or the status quo is bad? More of what? It doesn't matter. Just more. But, wait, what about the dream? What about the idea that, once we had surmounted the press of bare subsistence, we would turn to the higher pleasures? What about that? Never mind. That's dangerous talk, scary, subversive almost.

All that counts is this: Find the niche, find the potential consumer, design something, produce it, sell it, and to hell with its ultimate value to civilization. The eternal questions of truth, beauty, and justice can wait. The critical issue is whether those sweaty palms in the lobby of the Target store will move down the aisle and grasp whatever it is that was produced.

Tom Peters, author of the widely read books *In Search of Excellence* and *Thriving on Chaos,* has a series of television programs where he discusses the wonders of modern business. Particularly, he likes the notion of time. He likes compressed time, hurry-up time, decreased order cycles, telecommunications, and anything else that gets things done faster.

He actually launches into croaking chants of "TIME! TIME! TIME!" And in the large and attentive audience listening to him are people in nice suits and nice dresses, with vacuous smiles on their faces. Grown-ups, at least chronologically, who clutch his every word, who nod their heads in understanding and agreement, and who apparently never ask: "What for? To what end?"

Watching all of this, my gut tightens and my hope for civilization wanes. Never once, for he cannot afford it, does Peters ask: "Are we simply doing a large number of unimportant tasks ever more rapidly? Is this a large inverted pyramid where we use incredibly sophisticated devices to hawk fribbles people don't really need for anything resembling true happiness?" No, he doesn't do that. High priests dare not question the religion that sustains them.

Meanwhile, the Saturday morning television shows are busy developing more little targets for more little units. Later on, they'll take part-time jobs at fast-food restaurants to buy the stuff they're supposed to buy, wasting the years when time is most available for reading and dreaming, foregoing the pleasures of being young and wondering why the rivers flow the way they do and where they go. They are getting into harness, succumbing to what Loren Eiseley called "the mind-destroying drug of constant action." Nobody will tell them about the recent evidence showing the vast amount of leisure and play available to the old hunter-gatherer cultures, the cultures characterized in their textbooks as "primitive" and "subsistence."

Well, then, if this is such a good way to do things, how come we're fighting a drug war in our streets and gangs in our schools? And would happy people abuse their spouses and their children and the mentally ill and the elderly? What can be said about the savings and loan ripoffs we're all paying for now? And junk-bond kings with BMWs and hundred-billion-dollar fraud in government agencies? Working women are half-crazy trying to hold down jobs and take care of a home, partly they claim because husbands are watching video tapes of sports bloopers. Teenagers commit suicide, marriages are strained, one-fifth or more of our population is functionally illiterate.

The guy in the sweaty white shirt and suspenders, tailgating me at fifty-five miles per hour in going-home traffic, is talking on his cellular phone, telling a secretary to fax New York, immediately, with instructions to put the computer board in the overnight express so the computations in nanoseconds can proceed. What's he computing? Probably whether or not consumers prefer blinking red lights, or flashing green lights, or some combination of the two on a gewgaw. He got his data from college graduates in his marketing department who learned that "consumers need constant stimulation" and conduct focus groups to determine where the hot buttons are this year on the little creatures.

Now, nobody wants to say this, particularly politicians in Washington and the captains of trivia, but I'll say it: "It's not working." The population of this planet is going to be roughly nine billion by 2030. There are more than five billion of us now; that's twice as many people on earth as there were when I was eleven years old. The landfills are about filled, we are in the process of altering our climate, water is not only impure but getting scarce, we are in the midst of a mass species extinction, and nature is crying out from all quarters for relief.

But even if we were not confronting natural catastrophes, even if some technological wizardry could provide unlimited sources and sinks for us, even then we would have cause to question our ways. Why the level of despair that drives people to sniff white powder up their noses? Why do trashy romance novels, with some of the worst prose ever written, sell as they do? Why the violence? Why do we drug the elderly rather than caring for them? Why do we hold up material consumption as the goal and neglect our happiness as we do it? What ever happened to learning for learning's sake? What became of grace and beauty?

Anxiety is part of it, certainly. We are afraid, rightly so, of being old and poor and helpless. That can be taken care of. This country needs a security blanket, some kind of social assurance that, indeed, we will not find ourselves in such a dire position. The no-more-taxers out there, of course, wretch at such a possibility, for they see that taxes are going to be part of such a scheme, or maybe a reallocation of defense spending. Generally, these are people whose future is already secure. In some cases, quite a few, daddy fixed it up for them.

But all of this surpasses anxiety. There's more to it. And it takes on the character of a Greek tragedy, if you reflect upon our current state for a minimum of four minutes. We can see it happening, the results promise misery, but we can't stop it.

Frankly, we rip and tear at the fabric of nature and of ourselves because we don't know what else to do. Society withholds permission to be happier with less and to exchange consumption for personal growth. More than that, perhaps, we secretly have a greater fear of boredom than nuclear war. Probably with good cause. Aldous Huxley invented a drug called Soma for just this use in his *Brave New World.*

Narcotics is a kind of trap. People who take serious drugs have trouble escaping because the punishment that is the cost of the escape is perceived to be greater than the punishment of continuing to take the drugs, even though staying with the habit may mean the loss of everything, including life and family. We find ourselves, I suggest, in a similar situation in terms of how we're treating ourselves and the natural world and those in other places who struggle mightily for survival.

In other words, when we look at the options we see only insecurity and boredom and prefer all-out consumption and pure, mindless busyness to that unpleasant alternative. Okay, some of this is a little unfair. There are nurses and doctors and teachers and social workers and legal-aid attorneys, and others who are committed simply to making things better, and the pressures they confront are a cost of that commitment. They are busy because they are trying to deal with the problems of a staggering culture. So, as with all criticisms, present company always excepted.

We are living with a myth. Maybe an interlocked set of them. And myths have power, and myths can become lies. This is not a Norman Rockwell painting with gramps by the wood stove. Not at all. This is a culture that is floundering. We display more concern for the quality of our automobiles than for what gets out of them.

Recent surveys showing young people have no concern for helping others and little knowledge of democratic institutions or even an interest in acquiring such knowledge should not surprise us. They've been told, by symbol and by word, that consumption is all. Shuffling around in $125 sneakers with rich jocks' names on them will do that to you. (I'm sorry for continually using the sneakers as an illustration. It's just that I'm so appalled by, first, the fact that they even are available, and, second, the fact that parents actually buy them for whining little worshipers of people with decent jump shots and not much else, and, third, the fact that we choose to squander the wealth of this society on such trinkets while greater needs go unmet.)

This all sounds a little haughty, I suppose. Cerebral drivel from an elitist college professor who, himself, has profited from a growth-oriented world. That's the usual charge from those who live with myths turning to lies. But, for the sake of argument, let's say I'm right. Even if the mindless desecration of our culture and ourselves were not reason enough to change, consider the possibility that we are moving toward a time when the boundaries of nature are going to dictate some changes. And I'm pretty sure that's going to happen.

At some point, legislation born of natural or social calamities is going to alter our behavior. And we're not ready. What psychologists call "denial" is rampant. We are denying reality and living by myth because reality has all the appearances of being unpleasant. We believe the lies because we need to believe them. Thus, gasoline may well reach $2 to $3 a gallon in the next few years. It ought to be at that level right now if the market provided a true reflection of the costs incurred by driving, which it does not. That'll put a crimp in the one-car commute and the thirty-mile drive to the regional malls. What if the cost of electricity doubles or triples as we begin to deal with acid rain and other problems? Look for it. How about $30,000 for a basic automobile? We're on our way to that without the additional costs of high-efficiency engines and strict emission controls. Garbage collection and disposal unavoidably are going to become a major cost to us, in dollars and in time. That means we'll have to work even harder to buy the sneakers and all-terrain vehicles.

We have serious problems now, even with our wealth and our freedom to move about. What happens when we can't afford to escape each other? What then? Soma? It's not as bad as it might look. There are options. In Part II of this essay, I propose how to live with a less bountiful world in a way that is more joyful than we currently live.

Frontiers, Part II

We will be asked to change, as individuals and as a society. I'm certain of that, and I don't feel like much of a risk-taker in making the prediction. First of all, the natural environment, resilient and tolerant for so long, has finally begun to send messages that it's tiring. Second, unless we prefer to live by myths that steadily are taking on the appearance of lies, it's clear that we are not becoming anything resembling an enlightened civilization. Something is amiss, perniciously wrong, with the way we're living. The violence and drugs and intellectual lassitude are only a few illustrations of that.

It comes down, I think, to frontiers—spaces beyond settled regions. In this case, though, the frontiers are within us, not geographic. And our culture, along with our educations, have blinded us to the possibilities before us. The best way to see this is from the view of personal and societal decision making.

At any time, we confront a set of choices, personally and as a society. For example, as individuals, we consider various career options, a choice of residences, whether to buy a new car, whether to take T'ai Chi Ch'uan lessons or learn the fox trot, and so on. Call this our "choice set," the range of alternatives before us.

Our choice sets are limited, not everything can be done. Scarcity ensures that. I think of these limits as constraints. Our own mortality and the fact that we cannot be in two places at once is a constraint, time in this case. Other constraints are financial, physical, and legal, as well as social conventions and our own genetic abilities. Our choice sets therefore partition themselves roughly into two smaller sets: the attainable and the unattainable. The constraints are where the frontiers begin, the dividing line between what currently is available and what is not.

Within these constraints, just this side of them in the attainable set, we live in a settled region. It's where we are, at any given time. Yet we are urged, by our culture in general and the media and advertising and our peers, to launch tireless assaults on the consumption boundary, to push the limits outward, to acquire ever more in the way of sheer material goods.

To do this takes money, and money takes work. And work has its costs in not only effort, but also time. That's why time has become such a precious commodity in its own right; we have made it scarce by making it a cost of material acquisition. Moreover, the very act of consumption itself takes time.

But there are other frontiers, other places beyond the settled regions of our minds and bodies and spirits. And they share a common set of characteristics:

– They have a lower impact on the natural environment than high-intensity material consumption.
– They encourage personal growth, a plumbing of the richness that can be found in the reservoirs of the human mind, and human body, and human spirit.
– Some are within the economic capabilities of everyone; most require relatively little in the way of financial resources.
– They promote a craftsmanlike work ethic.
– They develop a "designing culture," in which all of us become sensitive to and responsible for the way our products appear and function.
– They result in a more discriminating culture, a society of

intelligent buyers, who disdain shoddy products and glitter.
- They foster a "learning culture," where the acquisition of knowledge and skill becomes a natural part of the daily cycle of life.
- Most of all, they result in personal and cultural growth, which are the areas most neglected in our lives as individuals and citizens.

Here's a preliminary list of such frontiers:

- Intellectual exploration
- The visual arts
- Music
- Writing
- Theatre/dance

That's not an exhaustive list. Certainly, there are those who seek higher spiritual realms through contemplation and other devices. And, for some, perhaps battering down physical barriers by participating in triathlons is enough. Then there are the crafts, such as woodworking. But I'll focus on the first four I listed, since they satisfy my two criteria: (1) they are areas I know something about, and (2) they lend themselves to individual practice. I differentiate between what I call the "personal arts," such as painting and playing the guitar, and "big art" requiring large numbers of participants, auditoriums, and heavy financing. Furthermore, fame is not the issue; participation is.

Do I want everyone to become an artist, or an intellectual, or preferably both? Is that it? In a way, yes. Not full-time, you understand, economic reality prevents that, but as something more than a spectator. I like to talk about what I call a *recreational level of competence* in these areas. And my definition of *recreation* exceeds dabbling. It means striving to work like a professional without earning your living at it. It means trading what I call *soft leisure,* such as gambling and spectator sports, for *hard leisure,* where we are active participants in our own development. It means traveling locally, acquiring the skills and knowledge to enter small universes with unlimited frontiers.

These frontiers, unlike the waste of our resources in the scramble for mindless consumption, are inexhaustible. As you walk into these unsettled regions, hallways lead to doors that lead to still more hallways and doors. It's mathematics, not just art, that provides the richness. Suppose you have fifteen different shades of color on your palette, and you're trying to decide which one to apply to the canvas first, then second, and so forth. There are 1.3 trillion possibilities here. Hallways and doors and hallways.

And the library is there. Pursue the problem of infant mortality in Third World countries. Become the resident expert, and present talks on your findings. Contrary to the myths perpetuated by academics, you do not need a Ph.D. and research funding to become a competent scholar.

Paint, and enter your paintings in local art shows, or just share them with your friends. Become proficient at Mississippi Delta blues guitar or old-time mountain banjo. Draw. Play. Work at poetry. Write essays or columns for your newspaper. Make your head thunder with ideas, your hands unable to resist the paint and the brush and instrument and the pen. Such thunder is not available for purchase at the mall.

Now, imagine an entire society committed to personal growth in areas demanding a craftsmanlike ethic. I can tell you this: the athletic stadiums would be empty on autumn Saturdays. A mind full of rich alternatives cannot bear the tedium of watching men push each other around on a chalk-marked field. It's just too damn boring, relative to other possibilities.

Would such a culture be able to compete in the world economy? We'd dominate it. Nothing competes with craftsmanship and intelligence. Those are the true antecedents of excellence. Period.

Would such a culture exhibit less violence? Less drug usage? Less child abuse? I don't know for sure; those are areas in which I lack detailed knowledge as to cause and effect. Still, something tells me that the answer would be yes. In addition to what I mentioned earlier, the arts have a way of exorcising the demons. That's a common theme in descriptions by writers and artists of why they choose to work in the arts. In addition, it seems clear to me that a fair amount of the emotional malaise I see is connected to the pressures of high-intensity consumption. Getting ahead has its costs.

About this time someone's going to raise a hand and point to the drug usage among musicians and artists. The last time I saw a ranking, which I admit was a while ago, musicians and artists were pretty far down the list. Doctors and nurses were at the top.

I'll grant you, the arts and intellectual activities have their frustrations, part of which is due to the lack of acceptance by the larger culture. But, if the culture at large is pursuing the arts, I expect such frustration would ease a bit. Furthermore, I don't happen to think all artists are among the truly wonderful. The arts alone are not enough, and I don't mean to imply that. I'm talking about the arts as part of a larger life.

So why aren't we all painting and writing poetry and playing music and studying Third World infant mortality? This is where it gets perverse. We aren't because we aren't. It's another one of those cycles, sometimes called vicious circles.

If children were taught, beginning in our homes and elementary schools, to pursue the arts and respect intellectual endeavor, and if this education were continued throughout high school, and adult life too, with applause and support from the wider culture, then we would have a society of artists and musicians and thinkers. We would have a culture of craftsmen.

But the attention given to the arts in our public schools, let alone in our lives, is pathetic. In spite of our professed concerns with education, the same is true of intellectual pursuits. We view the schools as training grounds for careers rather than as places where the pleasures of the intellect are developed. Those who think for the sake of thinking are to be distrusted and are the first to go when totalitarians strive for dominance.

A recent survey of 15,200 U.S. school districts showed only 53 percent of seventh and eighth grade students enrolled in art classes. Most of these were in general music, and we all know what general music classes look like. It gets worse at the high school level. Overall, less than 4 percent of the school day is devoted to the arts.

In terms of music, marching band is of no help. If it weren't for sports, band instructors would be in the same position as the visual arts teachers when it comes to support. I try, but fail, to imagine a thirty-seven-year-old person sitting at home in the evenings playing the "Washington Post March" on a trombone and being entertained by it. I can't get the image.

But I can easily imagine that same person working out one of Robert Johnson's blues licks or struggling to master a piano sonata or playing "Shady Grove" on the Appalachian dulcimer. Anybody recall instruction dealing with blues guitar or the Appalachian dulcimer in their schools? Nope. Those instruments don't work in marching band.

The arts, particularly the personal arts, are neglected. Universities are no better in this respect than elementary and secondary schools. University students are not required to demonstrate a level of competence in one of the artistic areas before graduation. That's in spite of claims in university catalogs about "educating people for life," claims swallowed only by naive prospective students and their equally naive parents. Worse yet, through entrance requirements emphasizing mathematics, science, and languages, universities deprecate the importance of art and music education in the elementary and secondary school systems. College professors, you see, also are stunted in their growth, limited to practicing only a narrow, left-brained kind of intellectualism.

Now, I have a recurring dream, and it goes like this. Students finish the written portion of the ACT or SAT examination. All the good linear, analytical skills have been demonstrated. The proctor stands, crumbles up some sheets of colored paper on the desk, throws a few sticks and bottles on the pile, and says: "It's time for the arts portion of the examination. You have two hours in which to create a work of art based on what I have placed on the desk. Clay, drawing paper, cameras, pencils, paint, and everything else you need have been provided. Those interested in music will be given a two-measure theme from which to work on their impressions. Poets can develop written works about the objects up here."

That's my dream. And I can assure you of two outcomes if it were reality. First, the distribution of scores on the exams would shift, since those with artistic skills would now have more equal footing in terms of overall results. Second, the arts suddenly would receive increased attention in school systems. The arts do not involve multiple-choice questions, and life itself is an essay or a poem or a painting or a musical composition, not a multiple-choice examination.

Back to frontiers. The frontiers we pursue determine what we think about. If high-intensity consumption is the dominant frontier, then considerable effort will be devoted to that. We don't think about other options because they are not in our choice sets. And they are not in our choice sets for several reasons.

Most of these reasons are cultural. Somewhere, sometime, we convinced ourselves that the arts are for the effete, best left to women and those men whose sexual preferences are viewed as shaky. I loved poetry and language in general as a young boy, but I soon learned to keep those feelings under wraps. In the milieu of my boyhood, where football and muscle counted, walking around with a poetry book was asking for nasty taunts and a thrashing at recess. At world summit conferences, the *men* plus Margaret Thatcher deal with real problems; the women visit craft fairs. Culture sends messages.

Another reason has to do with what we see as being useful. The emphasis on career training is so strong, and the contribution of the arts to earning a living so misunderstood, that poetry and painting and music are regarded as peripheral to life, pursuits for wealthy dilettantes. In fact, if we absolutely insist on being practical, a good case can be made that training in design and composition and other aspects of the arts are the best possible tools for workers and management in all types of enterprises.

When I need to be, I'm a pretty decent user of advanced mathematics. Yet, if I had to choose between my training in mathematics or, for that matter, my academic training in management, and my self-taught knowledge of the arts, I'd take the arts as more practical in the management of organizations and self-management as well. Though, I'd hate to be forced into that choice, and I see no reason why such a choice is necessary.

Design, decision making, judgment, composition, synthesis, and general sensitivity are the key ingredients here. Each semester I take my senior-level management students to the University of Northern Iowa art gallery where we examine the similarities between management and the arts. They always, always, are intrigued at the clear parallels between the two. For approximately 98 percent of them, this is their first visit to the gallery; they need directions, geographically and mentally.

It's amazing how we have driven the idea of the arts as being nonutilitarian into the minds of our young. A 1980 study revealed how elementary school children feel. They responded that they enjoy art more than almost any other subject, but, paradoxically, they don't think art is very important. Much of this has to do, I think, with the fact that we treat the arts as frivolous entertainment rather than as an essential ingredient in our eductions and in our lives. The kids pick up on this and view the arts accordingly.

William J. Bennett, when he was secretary of education, put it nicely: "Is it difficult to imagine that some children will first come to appreciate their own capacity for precise thought and economy of expression not simply in literature and science, but in the beauty and grace of art?" And Jacob Bronowski, in *The Ascent of Man,* argues, "Many great civilizations fail by one test: they limit the freedom of the imagination of the young." And, I might add, the rest of us, as well.

Then there's the debilitating notion of "talent." Some have it, we are told, and some do not. Nonsense. It's true that prodigies exist and struggle to the top through the sheer force of their gifts. But each of us can become at least competent in one or more of the areas I listed. Then we can appreciate, without envy (well, maybe a little envy), the work of those truly gifted, without denigrating our own efforts. Teachers, I'm sorry to report, have a hand in encouraging this view of natural talent as being essential. That's because they, too, have been corrupted, in spite of their early dreams, into believing that career training is the paramount task of the schools. Personal frontiers, not money, are what I'm talking about.

We are concerned with the decline of America as a world economic power. In the contemporary global economy, creativity, invention, innovation, design, and aesthetic judgments of all kinds are critical. The arts encourage each of these far more than extra courses in finance or accounting.

In a society where conformity rules, artists are seen as dangerous, which provides another cultural drag on art education. Artists forever are pushing at the boundaries I talked about earlier. That's called exploration of new and unsettled areas. Some of their explorations are disturbing, particularly to a culture that has little understanding of how artists work and think.

Recently, something of a furor arose around an exhibition of photographs by Robert Mapplethorpe, who died of AIDS. The photos that depicted homosexual practices of a sadomasochistic nature were particularly distasteful to many people. Senator Jesse Helms, one of the prime guardians of American myths turning to lies, was particularly incensed and is attempting to pass legislation severely constraining all artistic expression.

I found Mapplethorpe's work ugly and disagreeable myself, but I also understand the agony from which it emerged. It was a dying man's venture into unsettled areas. Nothing more. And I found the movie *Robocop* equally distasteful with its incredible violence. And I find big-time football to be in the same category as Mapplethorpe's photography.

Though I might try, I cannot be as eloquent about the role of art in a person's life as Jim Duncan, a sixty-five-year-old man from Cedar Rapids, Iowa. One autumn morning, over breakfast at the Mason House Inn in Bentonsport, I talked with him about art. Duncan spent his working years as a paperhanger and housepainter. Heart and stomach problems caused him to retire early, leaving him with a sense of not contributing to society, of being "a fifth wheel," as he calls it.

Art was something he was interested in as a boy, but cast aside as impractical. Courses in drawing and sculpture at Kirkwood Community College got him under way again, and he began to pursue watercolor and oil painting. The following words are his:

> Each [painting] you do, or darn near each one you do, seems to be a little better than the last one. You look back a couple of years at some of the things you've done, and you can see where you're progressing, where you're seeing more than you did see.
>
> I'm going down the road, I pull over and watch the clouds. You look at the telephone poles, you look at the ceiling tiles, you look at the insects along the sidewalk, the cracks in the stone, the grass, and I never would have believed you could get so immersed in looking at these things.
>
> I saw a shed down here a couple of months ago, did a drawing of it and then a watercolor of it when I got back home. They accepted it at the National Cattle Congress. It didn't win any prizes, but it made the show. That's progress. And, so, I can't be too bad . . . so you're starting to feel worthwhile.
>
> I'll probably never be a great artist, but the thing that gets me is . . . this morning . . . the heron out there and the reflections last night and the sound of the rapids, and everything. It's everywhere. That's how I'm going to die: driving down the highway, looking at this barn, and hit this flaming gasoline transport and die happy.
>
> Well, anyway, the thing that surprises me is that most of my life, if anybody asked me what I was, I would tell them a painter and a paperhanger. I've only been doing this [art] for a very short time, and I think I've found out what I am, who I am. If anybody asks me now, I tell them I'm an artist. I'm not a real good one, but that's who I am.

The personal arts carry within them the element of surprise, astonishment at what is out there and the magic that can be made of it. Jim Duncan of Cedar Rapids, Iowa, has discovered that. He understands that art is the vehicle for chasing down that elusive thing I call a "personal vision." Plato spoke of "the fair and immortal children of the mind." Jim Duncan knows exactly what Plato meant.

For, in the end, we practice the arts, not to improve our technical skills or work habits, but because of what they tell us about ourselves and about the universe we inhabit. Through our writing and painting and music, we explore the inexhaustible frontiers, the unsettled areas where truth and beauty and grace reside. And we come to see that, matched against the fair and immortal children of the mind, the trivia of material consumption and popular entertainment have no chance.

"Born to Shop," the bumper sticker, is the most tragic statement of our human condition I can possibly imagine. Though marketers undoubtedly applaud that ghastly self-incrimination, that implicit admission of having given oneself over to cheap and transitory and ultimately meaningless pastimes, I take it as a signal of an empty life and, more generally, of a society about to capsize.

Such a proclamation is clear surrender to the forces of environmental destruction and liquidation of the human spirit. Born, yes, but not to shop. Born to create and explore and think and leave something more behind than auctioneers holding up tattered doodads for a snickering crowd as the bidding tops off at a quarter.

It's time to stop running quite so fast and start the long and exhilarating exploration of frontiers that are inexhaustible. Empyrean frontiers that are productive, rather than consumptive, for ourselves and our society and our suffering planet staggering under the assaults of those who shop for life, instead of living it. In the end, along with Henry Rackmeyer's judgments, love, respect, and home-grown tomatoes are all that really matter. The arts can lead you to that understanding and to the possibility that heaven and hell are what we leave behind, not what we enter at the closing of our lives.

Drinking Wine the New York Way

Just when I was settling comfortably into my middle years, confident that I possessed a certain stock of savoir faire acquired from decades of living and travel, comes now Diane Roupe to remind me of how far I have yet to go. In one of those punchy and informative articles common to newspaper society pages, the *Des Moines Register* published a piece on June 29, 1988, that contained directions for holding a wineglass properly.

It seems that Ms. Roupe, formerly of Des Moines and lately of New York, has returned to her home, awaiting what the article labeled "career developments." While awaiting, she became aware that Iowans might not be handling their wineglasses properly and decided to set us straight.

And, I must tell you, it was a shock. There I was, drinking coffee at 6 A.M., awaiting developments in my career, and mulling over the choice between wearing my dirty blue canvas shirt or my "How 'bout Them Hogeyes" T-shirt, when I chanced upon the interview with Ms. Roupe. Stunned at the apparent deficiencies in my repertoire of deportment when amidst polite company, I read the article with near reverence. Nay, more than that, I was riveted by her words.

Then I immediately checked with Stanley Walk at the Sportman's Lounge in St. Ansgar to see if he had read and understood the instructions. He was smashing a hole through the wall of the establishment he and Allen Kruger operate and had difficulty hearing me over the phone. It turns out, though, he had missed the article and implored me to repeat the core ideas for the benefit of his customers. That, and my unceasing interest in improving the lot of all Iowans, compels me to provide here the essence of Ms. Roupe's wisdom. Now pay attention, this gets complicated.

DO NOT: Do not place two fingers and the thumb at the bottom of a wineglass bowl, with the last two fingers holding the stem. That used to be just dandy, but not anymore. This is known as the Marlene Dietrich Caress, and IT IS DEFINITELY OUT.

DO: Do place four fingers on one side of the stem and your thumb on the other side (never allow your thumb to stop touching the stem for more than five seconds). Such a grip prevents a premature warming of the wine due to your hand and also enables you to grasp the glass securely, according to Ms. Roupe. This is the Distinguished New York Authorities Clamp, and IT IS IN.

I know, I know, change is difficult. I whined at first, too. After all, old habits are notoriously hard to break. I learned my drinking skills from emulating guys such as Red and Corny and Zip and Lefty in my Iowa youth. All of them dictated, by example, the standards of proper etiquette to be followed while sipping from assorted containers in the bowling alleys and taverns of Rockford. Sometimes they were kind enough to offer exhibitions right on the street, usually late of a Saturday evening. And with only minimal persuasion, Lefty and the others would gladly move into more advanced techniques, such as the proper handling of quart bottles and gallon jugs.

Yet, Diane Roupe assures us that such a revision in our drinking manners is critical. She even manages to tie the new, and admittedly difficult, glass grasp into economic development. The syllogism runs as follows: Industry wants to locate in sophisticated surroundings; Iowans will be seen as sophisticated if we hold our wineglasses correctly; therefore, etc., etc. In other words, just wait and see if those silly old companies will move here unless we clean up our social act.

That piece of logic alone settles the issue and ensures rapid adoption of the new grip by all right-thinking Iowans. Remember Groucho Marx's duck that used to come down from the ceiling when people said the magic word on "You Bet Your Life?" That entitled the players to a bonus. Say "economic development" in Iowa, and the duck descends like the value of farmland after a speculative binge. The universities picked up on that right away.

But wait! There's more. Beer and highballs are out, and ordering either of those in a fine restaurant, according to Ms. Roupe, will definitely identify you as not being a New Yorker. I'm having trouble with this part. If a Brooklyn cabdriver goes to the Cafe Carlyle to hear Bobby Short and orders a Pabst, does that mean he's not from New York?

There are other things that will identify you as not being a New Yorker also, though Ms. Roupe did not point them out. Since she believes that people from Iowa will want to emulate the good manners of New Yorkers, I will provide several more guides for behavior when you visit the ol' Apple. For example, if you know the names and locations of all the states and have a fair idea of what transpires in each of them, you'll immediately be identified as not being a sophisticated New Yorker. This is particularly true if you know that Idaho grows potatoes. So, be careful.

Here's another example. You will not pass for a New Yorker if you dislike pieces of styrofoam pasted on yellow cardboard displayed in art galleries and selling for $27,542. Likewise, be careful of criticizing kitsch photography done in sort of an art deco style, featuring boring pictures of bored surburban couples sitting by bored backyard swimming pools. Be sure you like these photographs or you will be OUT.

Obviously, I'm joshing a little bit. We all agree that Iowans are not as well turned out socially as they might be, and there are serious questions that were not covered in the article. Here is a partial list of dilemmas that I hope will be answered in future interviews with Ms. Roupe:

Is balancing a wineglass on your nose or head okay? Or is that permissible only at the end of world wars?

Why are there sometimes two wine lists–one bound in leather and the other in plastic?

If you like to hold your glass down along your pant leg, what is the correct grip?

What is the proper grasp if you prefer your wine at body temperature?

New York waiters yank my wineglass from the table and pay more attention to other patrons right after I say, "Gimme a Bud." Why?

Iowans chill their wine to just above freezing. Does this have any effect on the right way to hold a glass?

How about those plastic champagne glasses where the stem detaches from the bowl? What is to be done here?

Why do busboys often err and put a fork at the top of my plate, perpendicular to the other flatware? Should I refuse to tip the waiter when this occurs or should I just cackle and point?

Why doesn't my van get better gas mileage?

Well, it's apparent that a whole new vista is opening for the *Register*. To paraphrase Galen Rowell, many Iowans come, looking, looking. And we need directions while we're looking, looking, so that we will never be mistaken for Iowans while mingling with the tonier elements of New York society. God forbid such confusion and its impact on economic development. Thus, we will continue to seek guidance from our newspaper wherein our arbiters of taste will instruct us in model behavior. The next article in the series will deal with how to keep score in tennis.

Oh yes, in line with this new thrust toward Iowa chic, Messieurs Walk and Kruger will begin offering wineglass-holding classes on August 1 at the Sportman's Lounge (students must bring their own glasses, preferably clean). I advise other such establishments to consider similar instruction if you want to be part of a future Iowa. The duck is falling.

I think I'll stop. Writing nasty things about such nonsense is on the same order of difficulty as nailing guppies to plywood and hitting them with roofing hammers. I'm sorry to be quite so blunt, Ms. Roupe, but I have other work. You see, children are dying in the Sudan from disease and hunger. Then there's acid rain, water pollution, soil erosion, the mistreatment of animals, child abuse, drug addiction, race relations, toxic waste disposal, the clear-cutting of the Amazon basin, students to be taught, and so forth. Besides, once the Arabs get their act together, New York will cease to exist.

But I am troubled by a single thought. I try to reject it, yet I cannot. In a world that pays so little attention to the things that ought to matter and focuses instead on the trivial fringes of what it means to be civilized, truly civilized, I must admit to the following: Diane Roupe is probably right. And God help us all.

Making Sense of Jesse Jackson

Jesse Jackson is a musician. Once you begin to understand that much, Jesse starts to make sense. When I first heard him speak in the 1988 presidential debates of months gone by, I kept saying to myself, "What is this man talking about?" I struggled for the logic in his words, could find little, and dismissed him as incoherent and unprepared.

And that was my error. Now I have learned to listen to him on a different level, holding the iron rules of rhetorical comment in abeyance. For Jesse Jackson is dealing with a whole different part of us. That's what makes Jesse work, and that's what makes him so unfathomable to those segments of society steeped in a distrust of passion.

A currently fashionable theory, and the evidence is not conclusive on this matter, has it that one part of our brain deals with language, with arithmetic, and with other linear processes. In right-handed people, these functions are controlled by the left side of the brain. The right side of the brain handles musical pitch, shapes and forms, and the strange, swirling particles of our beings that deal with anger and love and the urge for wholeness. Lefties are a little more complicated, but apparently they have similar partitions as well.

As I point out to my students, even if there is no such business as the left- and right-side functions of the brain, it is nonetheless a useful way of thinking about ourselves. There does seem to be a part of us that is logical, while another part, and an altogether different one from the first, is where magic resides. Jesse Jackson is tapping into our magical sides.

Several months ago, in an interview on Iowa Public Television, I tried, somewhat in vain, to argue that what Americans are looking for is goodness. We long for someone to take our hands and point us toward what we know is good and away from that which we know to be wrong and cruel and unbecoming to an advanced civilization.

We know it is wrong to pollute our rivers, to despoil our earth, to carve vast holes in the atmosphere by our rather natural indulgences in self-comfort. We know it is wrong to torture animals in industrial and university laboratories so that our unceasing advances toward better toilet-bowl cleansers will not be interrupted.

We know it is wrong to build weapons, more than we need and will ever need, while emaciated mothers hold dying babies in Africa. We know it is wrong for schoolchildren to demand designer clothing, for people to build million-dollar homes with swimming pools in the kitchen, while money is short for educational needs and for public assistance to the less fortunate among us. And, dammit, we know our society has taken a path so ill designed and wrong and predicated on the baser motives in our skulls that narcotics have become the solace for those who see no other way to peaceful dreams.

Jesse Jackson understands all of this, I think. He also knows that much of what troubles us is difficult to explain in the normal streams of logic with which we try to make sense of our world, a world so complex that the gods of truth merely scoff at our pathetic attempts. So, Jesse comes at us through the right side of our brains. And you don't have to be poor or black to engage in his call-and-response dialogues when he talks about funding social programs by dismantling portions of the defense establishment. Heaven protect us, Jesse Jackson is talking about morality, a concept completely foreign to the high-noon shadows that have inhabited several recent administrations.

Jesse relies on music rather than logic. Listen to him

talk. He reaches far back and pulls forward the old songs, melodies that speak of goodness and caring, of things we all cherish and have been asked to reject as naive, if not primitive.

He is criticized for his inability to keep the books straight when he operated PUSH-Excel, an organization he formed to promote education in the slums. That sort of complaint, in terms of his presidential qualifications, can only be issued by those who have no idea of what real management, real leadership, is all about.

One measure of a great leader is whether or not he has the wisdom to surround himself with those who complement his strengths and compensate for his weaknesses. If ledgers are a problem, and such matters are always an annoyance for true visionaries, the management of detail can be hired for a pittance. If he is prone to anger, then a cooler head should assist him. If he is given to impulse, then he should seek reflective qualities in his close advisors.

Jackson is criticized for his lack of experience. Lack of experience in what? If you can run a successful national political campaign on the relatively meager funds he has been able to raise, you know something about resource allocation. How about lack of experience in the political swamp of our nation's capital? That lack, if it exists, is probably a strength. We've been witnessing the virtues of Washington experience for some decades now, and what it seems to mean is learning to compromise one's dearest principles. I remain unimpressed with the arguments that such a resume is necessary for effective leadership.

Or, some argue, Jackson lacks political savvy. Well, he has over five hundred convention delegates, which says something about his political acumen. Gosh, even the gray-eminences of the Democratic party have breakfast with him now, even though they look a little uncomfortable over their collective orange juices.

Jesse Jackson is not a textbook on linear algebra or the niceties of Aristotelian syllogisms. He is the wind and the water. I still am not certain I support his candidacy, but I'm beginning to understand him, and he's starting to make sense on a whole different level.

The United States has been on a fast track to oblivion for a long while. Maybe it's time for a little more passion, a little more music, and a little less conventional wisdom. Maybe it's time for Jesse Jackson.

Getting the Words Rightly Set

There are mysteries, and then there is writing. When the kind invitations for talks to high school classes or teacher-training sessions or college writing workshops arrive, I provide a warning: "I know nothing about the formal constructs of writing. I had a terrible high school English program, a disillusioning experience with my only excursion into literature in college, and a communications skills course in 1957, which combined public speaking and some expository writing. That's it. So if you want technical help, I'm the wrong person."

"Well," they say, "come anyway and tell us how you approach writing." So I usually read from my works and talk about magic. Rhetorically, I ask: "Where do the words come from?" The answer is always the same and confusing to linear minds. "From out there . . . someplace. That's where they come from." Not very satisfactory in a society dedicated to formalism, to algorithms and technical knowledge in everything from sex to auto mechanics and undertaken in approximately the same fashion. Rule-based "know-how" is what counts in our culture, apparently.

Sorry. Writing is not that simple, not just a matter of rules. And, yet in another way, simple it is. I think of words and phrases and ideas as emanating from an inexhaustible bin somewhere. In my good moments, I'm grabbing things out of that container faster than I can type them into my word processor. When I'm really cooking, I don't even have to grab the stuff; it just flows onto the screen or into my tape recorder without, it seems, ever passing through my brain.

Here's an example. My wife and I were cleaning my daughter's room after she finished high school and left home. As we worked our way down through the layers of junk and salvage, I began to think our cleanup job resembled the work of archaeologists.

I walked out of her room, snatched a three-by-five card from my desk and wrote: "Excavating Rachael's Room." As we continued with the cleaning, the flow took over and wouldn't stop. Almost everything I touched with my hands and eyes became something useful—a metaphor or an image, a word or a phrase, an idea—for the essay I knew I was going to write.

The next day I sat in front of my word processor and wrote:

> Like some rumpled alien army awaiting marching orders, the brown trash bags hunker down on the patio in a column of twos. A hard little caravan are they, resting in sunlight and shadow and caring not for their cargos, the sweepings of a childhood and beyond.

That is the beginning of "Excavating Rachael's Room," an essay that appeared in my first book, *Just Beyond the Firelight*. All right, where did I get the idea for the essay on Rachael's room? Well, you might say, obviously it came from the cleanup job. That's a little naive, too pat. My guess is that millions of people have cleaned their daughters' rooms after the daughters left. Yet, no one that I am aware of thought to write about it, or at least to write about it in the way that I did.

And where did I find the simile, "Like some rumpled alien army"? As I said earlier, from out there, from the same place my songs come from, from the same place my photographs start. That's what I mean by magic. And that's one reason why I pursue the arts. I treasure the raw, visceral surprises that emerge from the creative process.

I once wrote that romance lies "just beyond the firelight,

in the corner of your eye." That's where the words and images and sounds are lurking also, waiting for you to discover them. In fact, those words I just quoted originally came to me while I was playing my guitar one night, working on a song that still is not finished:

> Just beyond the firelight,
> In the corner of your eye,
> Out behind your dreams somewhere,
> Underneath a winter sky,
> She is wearing golden earrings
> And a scarlet floor-length gown,
> And taking the combs from her hair,
> She slowly lets it down.

So I lifted the words from an unfinished song when I was writing an essay about the importance of romance in one's life. Where did I get the words in the first place? Where did I find the idea of using lines from an unfinished song in an essay on romance? Magic. That's the source of it all.

And if that's too vague, too incomplete and frustrating, I know how you feel. In my early years as a musician, I would ask experienced players, "How did you know where and when to use that phrase you just played?" The answer was always the same, mumbled usually: "Ah . . . man . . . I don't know . . . I just do it." In those days I thought the players were hiding something from me. Now I know better. They were reaching into that bin I talked about before, and the process has something to do with magic.

Talking about magic is a little dangerous. Too much analysis and it goes away. Magic is like love in that respect. But I'll try to say a little more, try to hang on to the idea of magic and, at the same time, say something useful about writing.

I think about thinking in three stages: idea generation, idea analysis, and idea synthesis. This is one of the most important concepts I know, and I didn't learn it from writing or from teachers of writing. I learned it from my studies of how best to assault complex social and managerial problems, which is another part of my life, though writing certainly is a complex problem of its own kind.

People confuse the three stages and attempt to carry them out simultaneously. But our minds are not set up to operate in that way. Sometimes, I admit, when the magic is really working, that seems to occur. Most of the time it does not, and to intermingle these three quite distinct and different activities of the mind results in confusion, a lack of conceptual clarity, and ultimately, an inability to get the words down on paper in a meaningful way.

So I have trained myself, and others through my teaching and consulting practice, to focus initially on idea generation. We are part of a society of critics, of people who can tell you what's wrong with an idea when it's halfway toward being born or, even worse, at the moment of conception. We treat our own thoughts that way also, prematurely discarding ideas that eventually may turn out to be valuable. To counter this, I slide into a noncritical mode of thinking. I simply allow the ideas on a particular subject to pour out of me, typing them down or dictating them into a tape recorder without considering whether they are good ideas or bad ideas or somewhere in between, let alone how I might eventually synthesize them into a unified whole.

Ideas are both cheap and precious. They are cheap because there are lots of them. They are precious because only a few eventually will turn out to have real merit in whatever project one is working on at the present time. So I generate ideas freely and without evaluation, knowing later on I'll do a critical sorting of them. After the ideas have been generated, only then do I pour them through an analytic sieve, deciding what the words or phrases I have written mean and whether or not they are appropriate for the task at hand. Following that, I'm ready for synthesis. In practice, it's not that neat. One moves back and forth among the various stages continuously. But I'm always aware of what stage I'm in at any given time and resisting the impulse to constrain unduly my set of ideas.

That's about as technical as I get in writing, except for one other piece of wizardry I discuss below. And sometimes, as I said earlier, it doesn't work that way at all. On those occasions, the generation, analysis, and synthesis all seem to happen simultaneously. A good example is the essay in this book titled "Incident at Sweet's Marsh."

I wrote most of that in nearly its final version while taking a shower. The shower door continually swung open and slammed shut on a March morning, as I ran dripping back and forth to my desk and note cards before good ideas escaped. I dried off and wrote the first draft of the essay in an hour. And that little piece remains one of my personal favorites. It just came along and wrote itself. Magic.

But it's not always that easy. "Slow Waltz for Georgia Ann" in my first book was horrendously difficult to write. So was "The Turning of Fifty" in this collection. And the short piece entitled "The Lion of Winter," also in this book, was tough going. The first draft was "overwritten." I had too much symbolism, too many attempts at profundity, and just too many words in it. But, though I tried mightily, I couldn't figure out how to simplify it. Finally, I let it sit for a month, got some distance from it, returned, and worked out the problems. At least I think I did.

There is one other technical device I use that cannot be explained in a general essay such as this one, for it involves a formal kind of mathematical thinking. It's called "structural modeling." This is a way of rigorously hooking together both qualitative and quantitative data into logical wholes. I'm good at it. I ought to be, since I've spent fifteen years using and developing portions of the discipline.

Structural modeling involves all three of the thinking stages I mentioned earlier. First, I generate a set of something called "elements." These might be factors in population control or agents causing the Earth's warming or simply random ideas for an essay. When the elements are defined and refined and judged to be useful in the task before me, I call upon structural modeling techniques to synthesize them. The latter stage involves using a verb phrase, such as "impacts on," to join the elements together into a framework that will guide my writing. The underlying mathematics ensure a logical consistency within the structure.

I seldom use outlines, since I don't think they are powerful enough to show the interrelationships among truly complex ideas. Real problems are full of such complications as feedback effects, where A impacts on B and B on C and, in turn, C comes cycling around to impact on A. Outlines are inherently hierarchical in structure, so feedback loops are difficult to handle in outline form. There are other reasons why I don't use outlines, but they have to do with the intricacies of finite mathematics, so I'll omit them here.

When tackling a really tough piece of writing, I often use structural modeling in its formal stages to get my thoughts clear and to get a preliminary structure developed that will guide me in my writing. At other times, I use structural modeling to test the coherence of what I already have written in a long, involved work.

For example, in 1987 I wrote an eighty-page essay, "Going Soft Upon the Land and Down Along the Rivers," which also appears in *Just Beyond the Firelight.* It's a complex piece of writing and thinking, for I was struggling with such ideas as economic development, the preservation and enhancement of the natural environment, the future of Iowa, justice, beauty, and how these ideas all fit together. In addition, I wrote it from the vantage point of a long canoe trip, and the ideas I just mentioned are intertwined with lyrical descriptions of the river voyage. The essay ran in eight installments in the *Des Moines Register.*

I sent the first draft of it to a friend of mine, Judy Sutcliffe, in California and asked her to read it. She wrote back that somewhere I had lost myself in the length and complexity of the piece and that it did not hang together. So I reeled out my structural modeling, identified the major ideas I had intended to cover, and ran an ex post examination of their linkages. Sure enough, Judy was right. It didn't hang together. I found the gaps, inserted necessary material, discarded some irrelevant ideas, and tied it together in a more coherent form. It worked, and worked well, judging from the response following its publication.

Now you say, "Aha! He does use technology; he's just hiding it behind the word 'magic,' keeping things obscure on purpose." Before you run off to pursue the arcana of structural modeling, however, I should tell you that most of the time I don't use it in my writing.

Why not? If it's such hot stuff, why not employ it all the time? In fact, people have asked me about applying structural modeling as a way of laying out the framework of novels. Certainly, it will work for that, if you insist on its use. But, for me, one of the main benefits of writing is self-discovery. I'm indebted to my friend, Scott Cawelti, for giving me that phrase, which, indeed, describes one of the reasons why I write.

And, especially in purely creative writing, I believe too much thought ahead of time about idea generation, analysis, and synthesis has a subtle way of destroying the process of self-discovery. In some manner, too much initial structure causes a kind of tunnel vision, with the result that serendipity does not occur as I move along. In other words, the magic gets suppressed by excessive reliance on a map so firmly drawn as to thwart surprise. That's also why I personally don't favor travel programs with fixed itineraries.

Generally, I'm more likely to use structural modeling on more or less technical pieces or articles where logic is the overriding criterion for the success or failure of the work. For example, I ran an informal structural modeling process after I had written the first draft of "Democracy and the Natural Environment," printed in this collection. Did it hang together on the first cut? Sort of. Not up to my personal standards, however, and I fixed it up a bit before I delivered it as a speech. For the speech on environmental education, also in this book, I built a structural model at the front end of the writing process.

For me, writing is not a chore, most of the time. I enjoy the strange, evanescent coming and going of ideas across my mind on their way to my fingers or back to the bin for future consideration. Call it therapeutic. Call it feeding the demons. Call it what you will. I like "self-discovery" best. I am discovering, as I write, what I really think, what I truly believe. College professors who protest writing requirements as part of the tenure process never seem to grasp that aspect of writing. When I write, I often find that ideas I once thought were tight and thoroughly worked out are, on the contrary, fuzzy and incomplete.

Beyond magic and technical considerations, good writing demands that you be open and attuned to the subtleties of the natural language we use for expressing ourselves. Somehow, you have to acquire that sensitivity. I'm not sure where I came by it. I was young, very young, when I started to feel it, I know that. My parents and grandparents read to me. My uncle, who was a nightclub singer in his early days and maintained a lifelong concern for language, talked to me about phrasing lyrics and matters of individual style when I was only five or six. Forty years later, he and I debated the correct pronunciation of "forte" over long-distance phone lines. I learned to read quite competently before I entered school. There were only a few books in my home, but one of them was a good dictionary, and the small-town library was handy. Though none of my family had ever attended college, a respect for language existed that got through to me.

And scuffling around the edge of adult society in a small Iowa town, I listened to the words arching out of taverns on summer nights when the doors where open, listened to the men invent new profanities to describe the pool shots they missed, listened to my mother's country relatives talk at family reunions, listened to my father and his fishing buddies discuss the rivers. Through it all, I grew to love the common language. I learned to love it for its meter and its color, its simplicity and its truth.

In the grain elevators and barber shops, in the Legion halls and cafes, a kind of moment-by-moment, subterranean theater perpetually is under way. The stories vary only slightly, the characters seldom. And at the center of it all is the language, clicking along in the roll and toss of daily life, floating and changing, evolving to meet the demands placed upon it.

Here's an example. My dog, Earhart Franklin, a child of obscure parentage, has his own language and signals me that a stop is required as we rattle through western Iowa in my old Dodge van. We are near Goldfield, Highway 3 in the summer. Standing in a meadow near the road, watching Earhart investigate a gopher hole, I notice a sign next to a country store: "All we have, we owe to Maury."

I grin and turn the words over in my mind, then say them out loud to myself, slowly, "All we have, we owe to Maury." What else can be said about this matter? Nothing. Parsimony has been sought, elegance has been attained. Without inquiring further, I grasp completely the passionate gratitude existing within that little store.

Earhart Franklin finishes his business and bounds toward me, ready for anything, as usual. I roll east, toward home, recalling something Hemingway said about keeping it simple, about writing sentences that are good and true. In Goldfield, somebody understands that. And, in my personal celebration of the language on that summer morning, I also am pleased that Maury is not forgotten.

Being sensitive is not enough, though. In order to write anything other than routine documents, you have to love the language. That much is basic. I startle my students by telling them I occasionally read the dictionary for entertainment. It's true. I do that. Here and there I find a word, jot it down on a card, and toss it in a box. Periodically, I review the contents of the box and type the words onto a sheet. When writing, I occasionally look at the sheet. Eventually, a word slips into my working vocabulary and finds just the right niche for itself in a song or essay or title for a photograph.

Here's a test of your creativity, and it's good writing practice as well. Open your dictionary to any page and, without looking, plop your finger down on a word, any word. Now, write a coherent article, essay, poem, song, or whatever around that word. Any word in the language can be the source for an interesting piece of writing all its own.

People debate the question, "Is There a Midwestern Literature?" I am disinterested, unequivocally, in such matters. I suppose that's what university English professors do with their time. I don't. I'm much more interested in writing than in talking about writing.

But, I do know there is a midwesternness in my writing. Don't ask me how I know; I just do. My midwestern heritage and environment have had and continue to have a profound effect on what I see and hear and feel and taste and smell. I know I am influenced by this midwesternness in the way I express myself in whatever medium I happen to be working. I look through the Midwest rather than at it. Rather like a special filter on a camera lens, you see.

There is something quite mystical, submerged and powerful, about this land out here that shapes and informs my work, and I suspect the work of others. Maybe it has to do with the climate and the surges of emotion it takes us through. Maybe it's the great flat spaces where you can watch a storm roll up an hour before it engulfs you in its power.

Or maybe it's a matter of distance. I do not feel or think about distance the same way that my Eastern friends do. A two-hundred-mile drive is nothing to an Iowan. People from Manhattan seem to feel differently.

More than anything, though, I think it has to do with quiet. Mostly, the Midwest is a place of quiet. There is space for the wind to be heard. You can listen to raindrops hitting country blacktops and mourning doves in your neighbor's trees. It's so quiet you can hear your own thoughts, listen to your own mind as it works, and you can catch the low murmur of the common language clicking along in the flow of daily life. It's easy to pay attention out here. But I imagine people from New York and Buenos Aires and Bombay feel the same proprietary way about the environment in which they live and grow.

When people ask me, "How can I improve my writing?" my answer never varies: "Learn to play a musical instrument, preferably one where you have to provide your own melody and meter and rhythm, simultaneously. The guitar, piano, organ, Appalachian dulcimer, and five-string banjo are all examples of such instruments.

Long before I began to write in any serious fashion, I was a musician, playing the guitar, flute, five-string banjo, and singing. And music, of course, has its own powers for saying what it is you have to say. Sometimes, though, matters of pitch and chordal movements and the like just get in the way. So I turned to writing essays and, later on, poetry. Then, further along, I moved into the visual arts with considerable intensity.

And I began to see that each of the three art forms overlaps and supports the others. For example, one measure of good writing is meter. Music drives the feel of steady meter into your very being. Now there are interesting musics and interesting writings that essentially are meterless. But I think it's important to understand meter before you decide not to use it. Learn to walk before you run, in common parlance. Besides, for me, the very best prose always has a strong sense of meter.

There is a difference between rhythm and meter in music. Most people speak of rhythm when they really mean meter. Meter is the pulse, rhythm is the time value of the notes played over the meter. Think about a song such as "Girl from Ipanema." The samba rhythm is subtle and intricate, but you can clap your hands in standard four-four time to the underlying meter.

Currently I'm reading a book on decision making. And God how I'm struggling with it. The author has some decent material, some things worth knowing. But the content is all that's holding me to the book. His rhythm and meter are despicable, absent in fact, and that's inexcusable for a college professor, particularly one purporting to be a writer. He needs to lay an Appalachian dulcimer across his lap for a year or two and then start writing. The difference, I'm confident, would be noticeable.

Meter is controlled by the way your words flow or don't flow. Without it, there is no underlying pulse to the writing—you can't tap your foot to it, so to speak. A lot of my students write that way. Yet, focusing on meter alone produces writing of the "See Dick run" genre. That sort of prose has meter all right, but it's incredibly tedious, plodding along like the work of a drummer on a Roman galley, keeping the oarsmen synchronized. Rhythm rides on top of meter, providing variety and interest.

Rhythm is manipulated by word choice, sentence length and construction, punctuation, and other such stylistic devices. Sometimes I use incomplete sentences in my writing to provide a kind of syncopation. A one-word sentence can function just like the quick snap of a drummer's rim shot. Here's an illustration from an essay of mine called "Jump shots," where I used a one-word sentence followed by an incomplete sentence for just that effect:

> Bored with school and small life at thirteen, I have decided to become a basketball player. Absurd. Five feet two inches tall, 110 pounds.

Music has other roles to play in writing. One of them is appreciation of sound, development of the ear. Writing has an aural dimension to it, though many people do not understand that it does. I read all of my writing out loud. Well, most of it. Usually I read to myself, but sometimes I try it out on someone else if I'm uncertain about the sound of a particular passage.

In addition to sound, I believe the language has tactile properties. I like the feel of certain words as they come across my tongue—"blue," "magenta," "tintinnabulation." When I test my students to see if they understand the feel of language, most of them are embarrassed. "All right, everybody, let's say 'blue' together and see how it feels." Feet shuffling, eyes cast downward, they are uneasy experiencing the touch of their own language.

You'll find me at my computer mumbling away as I write. Quite simply, I love the sound of language, and I like the tactile sense of certain of my writings more than others. This particular essay, as written here, is meant more for silent reading than speaking, though it works well as an oral presentation. Compare it with other essays in this collection, such as "Southern Flight" or "One Good Road Is Enough" or "I Am Orange Band," and you'll see what I mean.

Finally, music stirs something in my very being that causes me to want to put good language down on paper. This is part of the magic, part of being alive. Somehow I am carried along by the music, and I'm able to think of things to say and to say them in ways that I know I cannot without the music. I don't write to music all the time. It depends on what I'm doing. I have a certain sense of when I want to write to music and when I don't. Again, that's part of the magic I have learned to trust.

I came to the visual arts as an active participant fairly late in my life. I had this rather vague feeling that some of what I wanted to say was not getting out through writing and music. The natural language is linear; it comes toward you in a straight line, whether you read it or listen to it. But a photograph or a painting or a sculpture or a piece of pottery comes at you all at once, in its totality. So I began to explore the visual side of myself, mostly out of frustration. I felt there were shapes and forms and colors that I wanted to express and that I needed a visual medium to capture these. Having decided that, I immersed myself in photography.

As with music, I began to understand that the visual arts have their own contribution to make to writing. You hone your sense of composition, of symmetry and asymmetry. Notions of depth and texture become important. You become more aware of the ideas of "close up" and "far away." You develop much greater sensitivity to light, to the seasons, to the hundred different colors of a single leaf as the sun moves across it during the day and where the sun rises and sets in each season, where moonrise can be found in October just above a house in southern Iowa.

Moreover, for a long time I have been aware of the role that visual images play in writing. If you can see an image clearly in your mind, you probably can write about it. The visual arts increase this ability to form and manipulate such mental images.

Slowly, I have come to the realization that what I'm really doing is chasing down a rather elusive idea, the idea of a "personal vision." In my case, at least, this search must be indirect. The vision does not yield to a frontal assault. So my ways have become slanting ways, and that's where the arts enter all of this. For I now understand that the vision may never emerge in its totality, but in the search for it, I am discovering myself.

Writing is part of that search, as are music and the visual arts. Slowly you begin to grasp that process is what counts; destination becomes secondary. I see myself before a giant canvas, scraping away layers of accumulated paint, underneath which lies the complete vision. I am working only on a corner now, scraping, but I find myself unfolding in the process.

Eventually, I will create a work of writing joined, in a slanting way, to a series of photographs, all of which will be married, in a slanting way, to music that I will compose. That will complete my personal three-part cycle of expression. Writing, the visual image, and music will each support the other, and together they will become something more than their elementary sum.

Beyond all of that, writing is damn hard work, much of the time. That sounds like a contradiction of what I said earlier about it not being a chore. There's a difference between hard work and pure drudgery, and that's what I'm talking about here. So, what are the day-to-day routines that foster good writing?

First, I write a lot. Period. Articles, songs, essays, letters, poetry, and so forth. Not all of it's good; some of it's bad. When I look at certain pieces I wrote only a few years ago, I'm a little chagrined to think I let others see them. Yet I am unapologetic, for I recognize that failure is part of growing; every artist understands that much. And practice, which is what I'm doing much of the time when I'm writing, certainly is part of growth. I learned that from music. Practice develops technical facility, which, in turn, brings freedom with it. As I like to put it: "Good art rides on good technique." The enduring problem, however, is not to let technique get in the way of art.

Reading works of authors who know how to use language also is important in learning how to write, in the same way that listening to good music or studying the masters of photography help in those fields. I must admit, though, there are not many writers I like to read. Virginia Woolf is one of the best pure stylists I've come across. So is Thomas Wolfe, in a slightly flamboyant way. In general, but not always, I like Hemingway. I abhor his celebration of machismo and the killing of animals for sport, but I do admire his craft.

In terms of both style and content, Loren Eiseley is my hero, and I go back to his works over and over again, particularly when I'm in need of a little push. In certain moods, I pull Barry Lopez or R. M. Rilke or W. B. Yeats from the shelf. There are others, but not many.

Along with all the rest, there is no substitute for a teacher who says: "You will go no further until you learn to write." I had a teacher who said that and meant it. I have adopted his tactics, harsh as they seemed to me at the time. As I tell my students, "Think of me as a sheer, ten-thousand-foot cliff you must climb before leaving the university." I can count on a reasonable decline in class size immediately following that announcement.

Legend has it that I once poked a hole in a student's paper with my finger, while emphatically jabbing it and telling him that in spite of his good high school English marks, he was not a competent writer. The legend, in this case, is true. The student, a male, began sobbing and said I was calling him dumb. I was not. Incompetent is not the same as dumb, I pointed out, but he remained unreceptive to that slender distinction and looked dolefully at the hole in his paper.

And detail. That's a key ingredient of good writing. One of the reasons people write poorly is that they have nothing to write about. Knowledge is needed, detailed knowledge, and that requires not only living, but also research. Without believable detail, writing lacks a certain sense of conviction—it doesn't ring true. Detail is what makes a novel or an essay believable.

Your reader responds to detail, almost subconsciously, by saying, "Yes, that has a ring of truth to it; it feels right." Your readers usually will not have had the same experiences as you, so if you are to take them with you in your writing, you must provide enough detail to let them feel and taste and hear what you felt and tasted and heard. After reading one of my essays, people often will tell me, "I felt as if I was right there with you." When that occurs, I know I have done my job.

Library research might be part of your work. Other times, you need to go out there and see for yourself. A fair amount of prose I come across, and quickly reject, has the fume of what I call "armchair" writing. I simply don't believe the writer understands what he or she is talking about. When I write about Bangkok humidity or the sound of foghorns on a Sunday morning in Acadia or the color of a New Mexico twilight, I can make it live because I have lived it.

Sometimes your readers will have had an experience similar to the one you're writing about. In that case, it's the writer's task to make them say, "That's the way I felt, exactly, but I couldn't find the words to express it." Many people said that to me after reading "Excavating Rachael's Room."

Then there's the matter of craftsmanship. I think of writing as very much like producing a fine piece of handmade cabinetry. The same care in materials selection, the same care in construction, the same care in finishing goes into writing as that used by the master woodworker. After all, the idea is to create something lasting.

And that's where revision comes into play. Revising your work is the equivalent of the master woodworker cleaning up the flaws, carefully and lovingly applying the lacquer, rubbing the wood by hand, and even starting over if necessary. Students, especially, seem to believe, with enormous arrogance I might point out, that the first draft of their writing is acceptable. It is not.

I estimate that 50 percent, probably more, of my writing time is spent in revising. And, a good slice of this labor involves taking things out rather than putting them in (I just did that in this sentence). My students seem to proceed in the opposite fashion. They obviously believe that quality is directly proportional to verbosity and sentence convolution.

Personally, I find the work of revision more satisfying than writing the initial draft. That's where I really can get down to fine-tuning and use my creativity. Insert a new word, turn a phrase around, delete all the excess *that*s, toss out a paragraph and put in a new one. With the availability of word processors, the work of revising has become considerably less onerous than it was with the old cut-and-paste methods.

Where do you stop fussing with a piece? I don't know. Neither does anybody else, except for critics. There are two people inside my head. One keeps shouting, "Good enough!" The other counters with, "Do it one more time; you can improve it." I try to listen to the second voice. Still, as someone once pointed out, you never finish a piece of writing, you simply abandon it.

Lastly, and perhaps more important than any of the matters I have discussed, is the need for doing away with fear. It's a hell of a barrier to good writing in particular and to art and living in general. I can write because I am not afraid. That took a while to develop.

We tend to worry about what people will think of us when our feelings are put on exhibition for all to see. And good writing other than the most dismal and dreary academic work with a pretense of scientific objectivity or excessive pedantry, surely does just that. People say: "I feel the same things you feel, but I'd be afraid to say them in public." I don't applaud that attitude, but I understand it. And fear, the anxiety that comes from letting others see inside of you, is one of the reasons that potentially good ideas get thrown away.

After reading *Just Beyond the Firelight,* one man wrote me and said it was "an act of courage." I didn't quite see how that was true, but looking back through the book after reading his letter, I began to grasp what he meant. Not only was I highly critical of some powerful people in certain of the essays, but in others I exposed myself just about down to the core. I think it was in the latter sense he thought the book courageous.

Unless you're content to do nothing more than copy others and float in safe waters, risks have to be taken. And risk involves just what it says: the chance of failure or at least a loss of some kind. Maybe it's a loss of money, or respect, or perhaps it's leaving yourself open to the possibility of ridicule. Several of the pieces in this book are good examples of risk-taking. "Southern Flight" certainly is one of them, for it exposes me to smug and perfunctory charges of taking anthropomorphic liberties, if not purveying downright mawkishness. Those who believe they are superior to our animal friends always roll out anthropomorphism as they dismiss an essay such as "Southern Flight," returning shortly thereafter to their brandy, their ignorance, and the barriers to feeling and elemental truths they have erected around themselves.

That doesn't mean I'll love the piece forever. My moods and tastes shift, and the line between sloppy sentimentalism and true sentiment is a thin one. Sometimes I lurch over it. In a retrospective reading, I become aware of that. But that's part of risk-taking, and it's also why I choose not to write for a living, or, for that matter, to pursue any of the arts as a way of making serious money. Freedom of speech and the freedom to poke around the boundaries are, in many ways, the same as economic freedom.

"One Good Road Is Enough" also contains its own kind of dangers. That essay is a pure exercise in self-discovery, which I spoke of earlier. I had great fun writing it and absolutely wallowed in the self-indulgence of getting some secret cargo I have carried for a long time out of me and down on paper. In places, it's much like an exercise in abstract expressionism, and the reader can make of it whatever he or she wishes.

In a culture welded to literalism and the precision of microchips, that sort of writing is vexatious reading for some folks. It shouldn't be. Some of my photography has similar characteristics, prompting realists to ask, "What is it?" I respond simply, "It's whatever you want to make of it." He who tries to explain the Tao does not understand the Tao.

The need to overcome fear holds for all means of self-expression, even if you're not going to show the work to anyone but yourself. Your deepest feelings can cause you to shudder a bit, on occasion, because you didn't know they were there and writing has uncovered them. But the arts bring you additional freedom as payment for becoming free.

And that's the point of it all. As you begin to lose your fear, you will find yourself shedding even more of it. It starts to break loose and drift away in huge chunks, like ice off the Greenland pack. And then—then you start to unfold and see yourself. Overall, I think you'll like what you find, and you'll learn, rather easily, to live with that which you don't.

In Cedar Key, Harriet Smith Loves Birds and Hates Plastic

When Harriet Smith told her boss she was quitting her job and moving to Florida to write a novel, he offered her three months' paid leave and psychiatric help. By contemporary standards, his reaction was understandable. Harriet was selling $5 million worth of computers each year to high-level corporate executives. She was the personification of what is supposed to be the modern woman's dream, slugging it out and moving up fast in a glamour industry.

That was six years ago. And Harriet wanted neither a paid leave nor psychiatric help. She wanted to be free. So she chucked it all, sold just about everything she owned, loaded her ten-year-old son in a camper, and headed south from New Hampshire. She was running hard, escaping from a world where time is measured in nanoseconds, where worth is judged by the crackle of the bank check and the close of the sale. She never looked back.

Now it's late afternoon on the Florida gulf coast, and the long swamp grass behind her house turns a soft yellow-green in the fading light. Twenty feet away at her Cedar Key Seabird Rescue, brown pelicans recuperating from various injuries flap around in a large confinement. Harriet Smith leans forward, rests her chin on her hands, and says, "I want to open up people's heads and pour some things in there."

It took her a while to find herself and this half-acre in the Florida scrub country. She wandered around Florida for three years, south to the Keys and then north once more. By 1983, Harriet was living in Tallahassee, picking oranges and painting houses, doing some writing on the side. But the novel went poorly, so she tried plays and short stories, then articles. None of it caught on.

She drifted down to Cedar Key where the wild beauty of Levy County took hold of her. And, sitting on a bench along Second Street, she decided this was her place. While launching her painting business in a new market, she worked as a waitress at the Island Hotel, a place of quiet fame among those who seek gourmet food and similar comforts.

Harriet's Cedar Key Seabird Rescue started with an injured brown pelican on the beach. The story is a common one along the coast – five fishhooks embedded in various parts of the bird's body and monofilament line wrapped so tightly around a grotesquely swollen leg that the line itself disappeared within the swelling.

She waited four hours for a busy wildlife officer to respond to her call. And Harriet Smith, waitress and house painter, spent that time watching over the pelican and raging within herself at her own ignorance about what might be done to help. She remembers making herself a promise: "Never again, never, am I going to have this helpless feeling."

An internship at the Suncoast Seabird Center south of Clearwater gave her some basic knowledge. A correspondence course in bird biology from Cornell University added to it. But most of what Harriet knows about birds has come from the day-to-day caring for them. She disdains the more clinical, drug-oriented approach of many bird veterinarians and labels her approach to bird medicine as "holistic."

Harriet's landlord in Cedar Key initially was tolerant. But the birds and cages and dead fish and droppings in his backyard finally wore him down. So, now what?

The situation presented her with a moral dilemma. You see, when Harriet Smith left the computer business, she had made up her mind to be poor. "I decided that I always was going to be poor, that I was never going to own property, that

I was never going to own a new car again, never get a bank loan, and never have a checking account." When she talks like that, you can feel the foundations quake just a little, and folks in the chrome and glass houses along the southern beaches probably sense a sudden chill in the wind and wonder about its origin.

Yet there had to be a place for the birds. So she compromised a little with the system and scraped together $400 for a down payment on a small piece of land near Cedar Key. She makes her monthly payments of $83.68 directly to the previous owner. The tallyman again, but no banks at least.

Connie Nelson, friend and local artist, ramrodded a modest fund-raising push on Harriet's behalf. "Okay everybody, $5 each for Harriet's Seabird Rescue Center." Harriet was under way.

She built her own house, a small L-shaped affair, mostly out of donated materials. Well, "built" is a little too strong, too finished. The house is sort of emerging here and there as funds permit. The posts supporting the structure are not on the square, but that bothers her little. "My great-grandfather lived in a house like this; it wasn't square, it didn't fall down, and he was very happy. You have to get away from the kind of mind-set that worries about those things." Well said and noted.

"Everything for the house seems to come in $300 chunks," she moans. "Everything costs that much, for some reason." The next $300, whenever she accumulates it, will go for a well. For now, she hauls water in buckets from Cedar Key.

After that, maybe a better electricity setup. Her only supply of electrical power is carried by two extension cords running from a temporary construction electric pole. One cord goes to the house, the other to a freezer containing food for the birds.

But her private war against suffering is what really matters. She finances that and her own expenses by working part-time as a desk clerk in a local motel, by writing an environmental column for the *Cedar Key Beacon,* and by selling copies of her book, *A Naturalist's Guide to Cedar Key, Florida.*

As people learn of her work, donations trickle in. Some of the money comes from local folks, some from people in Pocatello and Minneapolis who own property in Cedar Key, subscribe to the *Beacon,* and read her column.

She spent $1,250 on her birds last year. She figures $3,000 a year would permit a first-class operation by enabling her to build better confinements, purchase higher-quality food for the birds, and acquire additional training for herself. Her monetary needs seem shriveled in comparison with the large government grants regularly handed out to academic researchers. Without degrees and credentials, though, she feels that kind of money is beyond her reach. "*Crud*entials," she sighs.

No matter. Harriet Smith is an expert at making do. Conventional thinking has it that high levels of purchasing by some swirling mass of procuring organisms called "consumers" are necessary to the well-being of the U.S. economic system. If you believe that, then you probably will find Harriet a little dangerous. By example, she is subversive in a gentle fashion.

Harriet watches the rise and fall of life in the marsh to the east through windows that were given to her. In fact, most of the house is constructed of scraps and discards. Sometimes she'll return home and find a used door propped on the stoop. Or the phone rings and someone asks, "I have an old water heater. Do you have any use for it?" "Sure, bring it out; I'll convert it to a solar water heater."

So what's the point of it all? What's it mean in the long run? Harriet is quick to respond to such patently stupid questions. "Most of the animals are injured by some human activity," she observes. "In some tiny way, ever so slightly, I tip the scales the other way. I talk about birds anywhere, anytime. People become aware of the birds, know their names, and call me when they see injured birds. Once that starts happening, people become more aware of what they've got here in Levy County; they realize how special it is."

She sees Levy County as one of the last few wilderness areas in Florida. "It's eleven hundred square miles, and it's absolutely fabulous. Essentially every habitat in Florida is here. I sometimes think, 'Fence off Levy County.' "

As part of her bird lectures and columns, she actively promotes her own brand of hard-headed environmentalism. Plastic is one of her favorite targets—she absolutely loathes plastic. "It doesn't work to tell people they ought to recycle and not use so much plastic. You've got to show them how. 'Here,' I tell them, 'here are five ways to stop using so much plastic.' I go to the grocery store and say, 'Don't give me those damn plastic bags. What's the matter with you, Harry? Why do you have those things?' " Fearing a full-blown lecture, Harry shakes his head and reaches for something else, anything.

It's early evening now, and the flashing cursors on all those computer terminals are far behind her. They blink somewhere in another time. Harriet feeds a small eastern screech owl recovering from a broken leg and an eye injury. The little guy's beak clicks rapidly in anticipation as he waits for her to prepare his ration of stew meat marinated in a vitamin solution.

While she feeds him, Harriet looks out across the scrub tree horizon. Out there, she knows, the white ibises, the yellow-billed cuckoos, the ducks and owls and eagles and ospreys and the rest are up against the power of a technology-choked civilization, and they are losing.

She knows that out there the birds are flying into utility wires, eating mercury-laden fish, and slamming into automobiles. And out there in the island rookeries and along the beaches, the wry and earnest pelicans are tangled in the trees and hobbling along the sand, fighting the fish hooks and monofilament line.

So Harriet Smith works through the Florida days alone. She's trying to get $300 together for a well. Trying to buy better-quality food for her birds and to find a home for a brown pelican with only one wing. Trying to open up our heads and pour some sensibility in there. She's trying to tip the scales ever so slightly. Not much, just a little bit.

(Harriet can be reached at P.O. Box 82, Cedar Key, Florida 32625. Her phone number is (904)543-5395, and her book on the Cedar Key area is $4.25 by mail or $3.25 at most of the stores in Cedar Key. She welcomes visitors to her rescue center.)

Spring Is Academic

They haven't changed a lot. When it comes to spring, midwestern students are pretty much like I was nearly thirty years ago as an undergraduate. They're suspended in a kind of climatic purgatory somewhere between the convivial lights of Christmas and the warming of the earth in April.

After the December holidays, there is an unspoken pact between the students and me. Here's what we silently agree upon: We will shoulder our book bags and march without complaint through the first eight weeks of the semester without mentioning the weather. Not one time will we mention it. The professor, however, is allowed to stand near the third-floor windows just before class begins, look out at the wet, and shake his head at the wretched tableau before him.

I have watched these months for nearly fifty years of living in Iowa, Indiana, and Ohio. And, unlike wine, winter does not improve with age. Quite the opposite, in fact.

Gray muck enshrouds Seerly Hall. Inside, the ceiling lights are bright and cold, in the way of modern lighting, like the wind hammering the north side of the building. I push the students hard, even holding an extra three-hour class on a Sunday afternoon.

You see, along with a modest retirement fund, twenty years of teaching have provided me with some wisdom. I know I will begin to lose the students, and myself as well, when the sun begins to carry the first hint of warmth. So, we're getting the hard stuff out of the way early.

We hammer onward for eight weeks. A little mathe-

---

matics is mixed with psychology and labeled management decision making. By February's end, I'm thinking of calling for mass, campuswide psychotherapy to counter the late-winter blahs. But we hang on, like ancient sailors in pounding seas clinging to the mainmast, and with the same faith in better things to come.

Then over the horizon flutters the first sign of hope, in the form of colorful travel brochures pinned to hallway bulletin boards. The words and pictures promise sun and sand, tonic and tans, and, somewhat more slyly, fast times amid the palms of Florida. The talk in the classroom as we wait for the bell deals with snow conditions in the Colorado ski emporiums and who's driving what twelve people to Texas in an old Dodge van.

The inevitable questions come. "Professor Waller, is it all right if I miss your Thursday class before spring break? A bunch of us are going to Galveston, and we want to leave Wednesday night."

"No, it is not all right. I have a marvelous lecture on matrix transposition prepared for that day." Then, softening, "Why do you think I dragged you in here for three extra classes on a Sunday afternoon in February? Yes, you may leave early for Galveston or Nassau or the moon, for all I care." I have frightened the lower 20 percent out of the class already, and the remaining students are becoming veterans, battle-scarred and deserving of a short rest before I whip them up the intellectual hills in one final April assault.

I look out the window during an examination period. Gray has turned to yellow. The snow is gone. Students are reading on top of our underground union. And like spring flowers from frozen soil, massive stereos have appeared on the front porches of fraternity houses. As I walk to my car, I am, of course, pleased that the boys have seen fit to treat us all to the slashing sounds of "Metallica" and other symbols of our ascendant culture.

Restlessness surges within me. The roads are opening, the sun is warm. I begin to think, "If the students can do it, why not me?" From my office I call home. "Georgia Ann, I've been thinking . . . how much do we have in the savings account?" I wonder if the old car will make it to the Gulf Coast and back.

The halls are full of spring-break talk. "Going anywhere?" "No, the damned dissertation, you know." I know, I do know well. I nod my head and remember Bloomington, Indiana, twenty years ago, when I was writing mine and spring was just outside my apartment windows.

The faculty is tired. During my seven years as dean, I learned, as with teaching, to get the tough work out of the way early. By April, the professors have had quite enough of complaining students, bad tenure decisions, and hotshot deans with visions of grandeur. They can see the end and woe be to anyone who stands between them and spring graduation.

Friday now. Gusty March winds late in the month and bright sun. Spring break begins. The station wagons and minivans with impatient spouses and motors running are parked outside the building waiting for the last class to end. The library is nearly empty, except for graduate students catching up on their work and junior professors slogging their way to tenure. The campus is quiet.

Living through midwestern winters is a little like the old story of the man who kept hitting himself in the head with a hammer because it felt so good when he stopped. So, walking to my car late on a Friday afternoon, I feel good. The undergraduates are on their way to Galveston or the moon or clandestine romance amid the palms. The graduate students will graduate and the junior professors surely will get their tenure.

Me? I'll work on my book for a few days. Then, I'm going to take the old Toyota up into the hills of northeast

Iowa and lie in the sun along one of the trout streams for an afternoon or two and remember, once again, why I love the Midwest as much as I do. Like a woman for whom the agonies of childbirth fade over time (so the common wisdom has it), by late March I'm already forgetting the winter. The flowers are blooming in the woodlands near my home, the creeks are flowing sweet and cold, the roads are opening, and so am I.

One Good Road Is Enough

Autumn in 1949, night, and the geese are moving south. I hear them talking, toss the covers aside, and scramble to the foot of my bed, looking out the window. Low they are, coming down the river valley and passing over town. On unsleeping wings they ride, long necks extended, with sober eyes that see only time and far things and space . . . and me, I think.

They know I'm here, I'm sure of that. Ten-year-old boys have not yet succumbed to a world counseling consumption in place of laughter and duty in place of wings. The geese understand. I clutch the bed covers to my face, responding to some curious mixture of delight in their coming and sorrow at watching them pass.

Celestial reckoning. That's how they go . . . by the stars. That's how they find the ponds of Texas. Scientists study their ways, dissecting and inducing. The answers will elude them. It's magic, and no one can argue me otherwise, at age ten or four decades later. Logic and data have their place, but not in the night, not out along the roads of wonder, where the music rises and the Canadas fly and a wizard waves them onward with long sweeps of his arm from tall grass in the river meadows.

I lie back on my pillow. My parents are asleep, but the little brown radio beside my bed, the one with only two dials and tan cloth covering over the speaker, glows in the darkness. "Welcome to 'Your Saturday Night Dance Party,' " the smooth baritone from New Orleans says. The music is live, and I know, absolutely, there are handsome men and beautiful women. They are eating and drinking, and dancing on a southern rooftop, a big hotel, their hair only slightly ruffled by a soft wind from the gulf.

Over the music and following the geese I hear a Rock Island freight train. In the bottomlands south of me, the wizard is laughing and does a backward flip, unable to contain himself. The Road is busy tonight—music from New Orleans, geese across the moon, trains across the trestle. The wizard loves the Road and is teaching me to love it, as both an illusion and a reality.

I fade in and out of sleep, wandering along the edge of things, open to the possibilities. The music changes and images come. People dressed in wind-whipped black, carrying daggers with carved handles and drinking tea in front of flapping tents, waiting for the call to prayer. Camels moving silk and frankincense at a steady pace over blowing sand, pushing hard toward Medina. Near morning, my mother pulls the covers over me and turns off the little radio, while I travel, far from her.

There was only one good road leading out of Rockford, Iowa, back then. The rest were gravel, loose and dusty in the summer, treacherous in the winter. But one good road is enough. I knew that's all it took. I could travel east on it, go south on Highway 14, swing east again and catch one of the big highways leading down to New Orleans, or, for that matter, to Paris or Persia or twilight places in the Amazon Basin.

These were not fantasies without the possibility of fulfillment. I never believed that for a moment. They were plans, you see, plans that could be converted into small-town sidewalks that turned into streets that turned into highways and the highways into old steamers or airplanes or caravans headed toward market towns. The steady two-beat of a New Orleans drummer could become the complex syncopations of wrinkled hands on tightly stretched goatskin in high-desert arroyos, and the Rock Island freight could some day be transformed into a long, chuffing train across Siberia. The images are the beginning; you must have the images first. Then comes the Road.

So I lean over a 4 A.M. hotel balcony in my forty-third year and watch Bombay work its way toward morning. Thirty-four hours in front of this, I had shut the front door of my house in Cedar Falls, slapped my vest pocket to make sure the tickets and passport were there, and picked up my suitcase. Car to the airport, commuter plane to Chicago, jet to New York, and there in the darkness was Air India 106, loading. Then London by daylight, and into the night again—Europe, Istanbul, Persia, the Gulf of Oman. India, unknown, and fearsome in that ignorance, out there somewhere.

On the balcony, I drink a Kingfisher beer as light approaches, watching Arab dhows run up their sails into the first wind of morning where the Portuguese once harbored, watching the street people cook their breakfast on charcoal burners, thinking of a little brown radio humming, geese flying, and a wizard promising me that my world would not always be so circumscribed as it was then.

I wander the streets of India. Touts offer sightseeing, drugs of any kind, and women, or young boys if a woman is not to my liking. I swim in a pool at dawn, listening to a flute somewhere, and fall in transient love with Indian women in green silk, gold upon their bodies. For seventeen nights I eat at a table next to that of Sir David Lean and his wife. He's here scouting locations for *A Passage to India.* We do not speak. My midwestern reticence and respect for privacy prevent me from asking about his dreams as a young boy. I know he thought of deserts and jungles and dark winds from Java, though.

And Arabia came along. On Themari Street in Riyadh, the old ways endure. There is gold, and women with covered faces and men with covered intentions. There are calls to prayer and desert winds, and I wander through the markets at night looking for presents to take home. The bracelet will do, and the necklace. The scarf also. I flag down a taxi in the middle of a broad avenue. The driver is a Bedouin who remembers the sound of hooves and the taste of blowing sand. Far to the west, Canadas are beating their way south over the rooftops of northern Iowa.

Then Munich and Dubai and Hong Kong and Paris and on and on. I ride a coastal boat south of Puerto Vallarta to a fishing village. Staying there for a week without light or pure water, I listen to an African drummer tell me how the drums can talk, if you have the skill. I believe him and sit nearby while he plays to the darkness, on a hill 167 stone steps above the village. In the morning a man from San Francisco sings his night-dreams and invites others to do the same, while another man murmurs incantations to the beat of a smaller drum.

In the river towns of Belgium, winter lies hard and brittle upon me. Moving across the cold marble floors of a Flemish cathedral, I listen to the sound of my boot heels and wonder if the bishops in their crypts of stone are listening also. Was this the place? There's something here I can't touch, some ancient sense of having stood in these shadows before, and watched. Watched the lady in silver, small hurried steps as she came streaming down a secondary aisle past the confessionals and toward me. The image is there for a moment only. It wavers, dissolves, as early light comes through high and painted windows and colors orange a suffering Jesus, hanging, crucified.

St. Maarten is expensive, but the beaches are good. You can make up the cost at the casinos if you know blackjack and the cards are running your way. I am suspicious, though, about playing against the government. Governments think of gambling as taxes; they have unfavorable rules and close the casino while I'm in the middle of a streak. The hell with 'em. I put my winnings in metal box at the hotel and catch the morning flight out of there. I'll try Macao next.

I ride long-tailed boats through the backwaters of Bangkok, hang off of foggy cliffs in Acadia with my cameras, and follow snowy egrets through the swamps of south Georgia. In Big Sur, I read my poetry by firelight. There are professional poets with long hair in wide-brimmed hats, and pretty young women who love the idea of poets more than the words. The high-plains drums are still there in New Mexico, if you listen, and old dogs lie in the streets of La Push, where violent January waves hammer the coast of northwestern Washington. A fusty woman, from Omaha twenty years back, combs the Oregon beaches and dreams of secret cargos only she will find. I spend an hour talking with her about that.

Now there is more than one good road out of Rockford, Iowa, though still only one to the east. The same one. I visit there and talk with my mother. She remembers the old brown radio, the one with two dials and a tan cloth covering over the little speaker. She remembers the late-night sound of geese overhead. But she never quite has understood the wizard or the Road or why the man she raised loves it so.

"India?" she says. "How many times will this make?" "Three," I say. "There is more out there, and I'm fifty now. It's time for India again."

At some point, it gets down to "lasts." It's getting there now. I wear clothes for a long time. I wonder if my leather jacket, worn but tough, is the last one I'll buy. And my boots, good ones, Red Wings, are the same. The man at the shoe shop says they're going to outlive me. And my old hat? And the guitars? They'll go on forever. Maybe this is the last of the India voyages. Maybe.

I go down into the bottomlands to talk with the wizard of my summers. His ways are slanting ways, as mine have become and turn ever more so. He looks at the river purling by and listens to my questions. I ask again about the geese and the Road and the music, and what it all means. Where does it go from here? What about the "lasts"?

He is a fey companion, uneasy with too much directness, and begins to move away from me through meadow grass, chanting as he goes, his voice fading:

The High-Desert Master gave me a child
In return for some footprints
I found in the sand.
And I carried him here
Through fall and through winter
  Past old riders turning their ponies for summer,
  Past slavers who cried for their right to the boy,
  Past dancers who moved through the streets of Castile,
  Past arms reaching out from windows and doorways,
  Past women in black who were crying and offered
    Their only true daughters for a sigh and a drachma,
  Past those who would counsel prudence and claimed
    The dancers had gone and no more would follow,
  Past old harbor seals who lay in the sunlight
    And remembered the coming of Christ and before.
I carried him here to sweet meadows bending
And fought off the bandits who tried for his soul.
I gave him his love of sails leaving cover
And the sound of old flutes on the first wind of morning,
  While I showed him the maps
  Scribbled in chalk,
Washing away on the walls of September.
But women in green, with gold on their bodies,
Ah, they were the ones who took him away,
And gladly I gave him
Asking only one promise:

  You must teach him to dance
  In the twilight of Eden,

In the moments remaining,
Before it has gone.
For he is the last one
And

"Never again," cried the High-Desert Master.

"Never and never and never again."

Looking upward, he begins to sing, sweeping his small arm in widening arcs. I follow the point of his finger. Geese are moving south across a daggerlike slice of moon, their ancient sextants working in sober eyes, taking them along time and space, toward the ponds of Texas.

I drive my truck out of Rockford, down the one good road to the east. On the tape deck, Kitaro plays of blowing sand and loaded camels pushing hard toward red-walled cities in the deserts of Rajasthan. Goatskin drums underneath the melody. Switching over to celestial reckoning, I jam my boot harder on the accelerator, drifting somewhere between illusion and reality, refusing to succumb, thinking of magic . . . and believing in it.

Managing Change: Getting from Here to There and Avoiding Traps along the Way

Condor Number Nine, the last of the California condors in the wild, was brought to ground in April 1987 and placed in a captive breeding program in the San Diego Zoo. About the same time, the last existing dusky sparrow died in a cage in Florida.

Parts of Ethiopia teeter on the brink of a complete biological collapse, India finds itself running out of firewood, and the clear-cutting of the Amazonian rain forests continues.

Along with all of this bad news, many Iowa communities are struggling with economic hard times, the loss of population, and dark threats about school closings due to reorganization.

Read about in the newspapers or heard on the radio or observed on television or discussed in educational forums, all of the events I just mentioned appear to have nothing in common except bad fortune. They all seem to be part of what William James once called "the great blooming, buzzing confusion" around us – a melange of curious happenings with no more apparent order than the meanderings of a yellow butterfly on a summer afternoon.

Yet there is pattern here, if you look for it. If you lay

This essay is excerpted from speeches given for the Grinnell 2000 Foundation, the Iowa Association of School Boards, and the Family Practice Residency Assistance Program.

upon these events the right templates, things begin to make a little sense.

All of these occurrences are the result of decision making. They are illustrative of Adam Smith's famous guiding hand run amuck. In each of these cases, people with mostly honorable motives, with generally good intentions, have made decisions according to a particular set of values. Examined individually, any one of these decisions appears quite rational, yet the cumulative results of many such decisions produces tragedy.

Moreover, many of these situations are not isolated—they are tied into larger systems. And within systems of even modest complexity, one discovers a certain type of phenomenon technically called "positive feedback cycles," which are more commonly known as vicious circles.

For example, economic decline results in individual decisions to leave a community. As people leave, businesses close and schools disappear. This only leads to more incentive for people to leave the community and for more businesses to close. And the cycle continues.

In general, what we are dealing with here is a set of ideas known as "traps." When more than one person is involved, as is almost always the case, such situations can be called "social traps." (I am relying here on some basic concepts and terminology developed fifteen years ago by John Cross, Mel Guyer, and others at the University of Michigan.)

The essence of a social trap is decision making under conditions of multiple but conflicting rewards and punishments. Such decision making is found in the literature under the heading of "multiple criteria decision making."

Here's a simple example. You set out to purchase an automobile. Your dominant criterion, your objective, is "good, solid transportation." Of course, there are other criteria lurking in your mind, such as nice appearance, fair price, good gas mileage, luxury, and perhaps prestige. Still, with jaw firmly set and a quiet satisfaction, maybe even smugness, in your common sense, you know that good, solid transportation is your main objective.

On the showroom floor or the dealer's car lot, however, strange things begin to happen. Your criteria begin to shift in terms of relative importance to one another. You look at the dusty 1984 Plymouth, which provides the good solid transportation you are looking for, out on the used car lot, and, with a little urging from the salesman, compare it with the BMW sitting all sleek and muscular behind the glass walls of the showroom.

The blandishments of the moment now begin to dominate. The need for "good, solid transportation" can be met by the BMW, and you also get a whole lot of luxury, performance, and the plaudits or envy, you really don't care which, of your neighbors. Besides, if you put off painting the house for two years, let the roof repair go for a while, and get that raise you think is coming, things will work out all right. Moreover, you only live once and you owe yourself at least some reward for all your hard work. On the way home, the BMW purrs like a fat kitten, and you hardly notice the peeling paint on the garage when you drive that dark green symbol of your success and good taste into it. You have just been trapped.

Likewise, the struggling farmer looks at the sheet or rill erosion on the back eighty, knows that a different method of tillage is necessary, but puts it off, just to get one more good crop to meet creditors' demands. And the Indian peasant knows that wood should be conserved, but there is tonight's meal to worry about. The problem with these situations is that the individual decisions about erosion or firewood have effects that extend beyond the single individual and, therefore, become traps that ensnare all of us—social traps. Erosion despoils our water supplies and cutting the firewood robs the well-being of others in the village.

Incidentally, if your purchase of the BMW causes financial strain on your family and, secondarily, the consequent emotional turmoil that usually accompanies such strain, you have converted an individual trap into a social trap.

Now, how does all of this relate to communities? It will help if you visualize two circles, one on your left and one on your right. Label the circle on your left "the way things are now." Label the circle on the right "the way I want things to be." Next, bring these circles together and let them partially overlap.

We now have a little model that helps to visualize what change really means. Change is converting the way things are now to the way we want things to be. Presumably we like some of what we are now, and in moving to what we want to be, we desire to preserve some of the present. That is what the overlap portrays.

But what I am talking about so far is managed change. Most of the change I see about me is unmanaged. It is, in the kindest way I can put it, "muddling through."

Muddling through really amounts to looking at the options before you at any time and choosing alternatives that promise rewards and avoid punishments. Most of us operate that way, and doing what feels good and avoiding things that don't feel good is a pretty decent way to get along for most purposes.

But, in some cases, important ones, this generally successful learning strategy leads us astray. When that occurs, we become trapped. Change requires decisions, lots of them, and a sheer muddling through strategy for a community likely will lead to some serious traps.

In its desire for jobs, a community may try to attract a manufacturing plant, any plant, and blinded by the promise of short-term rewards may find itself with an unwelcome corporate citizen whose mode of operation changes the character of the community. Jobs have been attracted, but at a considerable price.

Do you really want to cut down all the trees along Main Street just to put in larger sewers to accommodate the new plant? Is it worth enlarging the water supply system via increased taxes to accommodate growth?

Visualize once again our two circles representing the change process. Most communities think they want to be something else, but they have not defined what it is they want to be. I call this a lack of vision.

Without a vision, without a reasonably well-defined portrait of where you want a community to go, muddling through becomes the dominant strategy. And muddling through, which really amounts to doing what seems right at the time, can lead to traps. Part of this has to do with the uncertain nature of things. In turbulent times, pure uncertainty about future events can result in traps.

More often though, traps result from poorly conducted planning processes, from complex trade-offs among competing objectives, and from a lack of vision, for it is vision that supplies the important criteria for community decision making.

With all of this in mind, I turn now to the second part of this essay, three things to help you in getting from here to there and avoiding traps along the way. These are not great and lofty abstractions about communities. Rather, these are some practical suggestions for managing the process of change.

If I were allowed to choose only one thing to teach to people who are interested in moving communities forward, I would teach them how to run a meeting. Most of the meetings I observe are little more than cocktail parties without alcohol.

People get their coffee, sit down, maybe joke a little, and the chairperson calls the meeting to order and says something about the problem the group is to deal with. After that, it's all downhill.

Person A has something relevant or irrelevant, positive or negative, to say about the situation at hand. Person B either agrees or disagrees with A or attempts to build on what A has said. Person C sits there and says little or nothing.

Meanwhile, person D has been making some notes and injects an idea that leads the group off in another direction. Person A is mildly upset that D does not seem to be agreeing with his or her initial position, and B does not like D personally, so naturally D's ideas are to be dismissed. Person E is frustrated at the lack of progress and attempts to take the group off in another direction. C still sits there quietly.

The ideas get tossed back and forth, emerging, being discussed, and dying in almost random fashion.

Thirty-seven minutes have now passed in a meeting scheduled for one hour. But B also sits on another community board that is meeting the same evening and exits while making appropriate apologies. Person F never did show up. She later provides excuses, but her real reason is that nothing ever gets done at these meetings, and she's trying to figure out a way to disengage herself from this particular group.

People get more coffee, visit the restrooms. A joke about the current athletic season leads to ninety seconds of irrelevancy about athletics in general, and we are now at forty-nine minutes of the sixty-minute meeting. It's clear that another meeting will be necessary. In fact, that's all that is clear at the moment. So, the last ten minutes are spent trying to find gaps in personal calendars when the next meeting can be held.

Some of the most able people in the community are not at the meeting. They have been put off by the large amount of personal time required for such meetings and have cut back their involvement.

And there are other noticeable absences. There are no blue-collar workers or garbage collectors or poets or artists in the group. Instead, the group is composed of six reasonably successful retail merchants, a representative of the major manufacturing plant in town, one black from the local social service agency, one person from the nearby community college, one real estate agent, the executive director of the Chamber of Commerce, two lawyers, three housewives representing either their neighborhoods or service organizations, a professor of history from the local college, and the person from the League of Women voters who had to leave early to get to that group's meeting.

The adjournment of the meeting is cordial. But on the way home, most of the attendees silently wonder about the futility of it all. They have been meeting this way for six months and they seem to be no further than they were at the beginning. They are muddling through, and they know it. Furthermore, they eventually will feel pressured to make a decision, any decision, and it likely will be a bad one. It likely will lead them into a trap.

What's wrong here? First, the group is too large. Whoever organized this group wrote down all of the various factions that needed to be represented for purposes of pure democracy, added in those people who expressed an interest in being on the group, and included those who would serve as appropriate symbols of local power blocs. The head count is eighteen, which is about ten more than the maximum number for any group to be productive.

Second, ideas, like people, need to be managed. If the opposite of management is chaos, then that's what we have here.

Third, person C may have some good ideas, but he has been silent through the entire meeting. He's not very articulate in public forums, and knows it, so he doesn't talk. On the other hand, person A loves to talk and has just occupied fourteen minutes of the total thirty-four minutes actually spent in talking about the problem.

Fourth, there was no attempt to divorce ideas from personalities. People who are well-liked get a better hearing than those of irascible demeanor.

Fifth, there never was any real focus on the problem. Rather, there was a lot of shadowboxing around the major issues.

Sixth, there was no sense of resolution. People did not carry away with them any feeling of progress or any clear idea of what the next step should be.

Seventh, there was no documentation of what transpired. Minutes were kept and will be dutifully approved at the beginning of the next meeting. But the minutes only reflect the chaos of the meeting: "It was moved and seconded, etc., etc."

Eighth, ideas from important segments of the community were not heard, segments such as blue-collar workers and garbage collectors and poets and artists, either because they were not invited or because they feel intimidated by such meetings or, maybe, because they recognize that most of what transpires in such forums is nonsense and not worth wasting their time on. True democracy has been aborted.

Ninth, and perhaps most important, the generation of ideas constantly was being confused with the task of analyzing these ideas. The kinds of thinking required for these two necessary processes are quite different.

There is a way around all of this. For fifteen years I have been using something called the Nominal Group Technique (NGT). It is a way to bring together diverse people to work on a common problem. It focuses debate, allows for creativity within a well-defined structure, permits and encourages the contributions of shy people, absolutely shuts down soapboxers who dominate meetings, and produces results.

I have used the NGT and variations of it in tough situations from Waterloo, Iowa, to Kansas City to Richmond, Virginia, to Bangalore, India, to Riyadh, Saudi Arabia. It has never failed me once, whether the problem was one of small importance or large magnitude, whether the participants were rich or poor, Christian or Jewish or Muslim or Hindi.

The basic ideas of NGT can be learned in two evenings' reading from a book entitled *Group Techniques for Program Planning* (Andre Delbecq and others, Greenbriar Press, 1986). Practice the technique on a reasonably friendly group once or twice before taking on a nasty situation.

If the difficulty of managing people and ideas in groups is not enough, communitities also confront the difficult problem of *competing objectives.* In a given decision or discussion about a community's future, people likely are concerned about a number of important things: the tax base, jobs, water quality, air quality, parks, an aging population, support for the arts, services for the poor, services for the elderly, the school system, beautification of the city, salaries of city administrators, providing activities for teenagers, the decline of the downtown business district, the state of the city budget, and the condition of the community's infrastructure (sewer systems, streets, water mains, and the like).

Let me return to my car-purchasing example to illustrate this type of situation. When you purchase a car, new or used, you have several objectives in mind, such as good gas mileage, low maintenance, air conditioning, luxury, dependability, prestige, appearance, type of warranty, and cost.

If you have only one objective, the decision is relatively simple. For example, suppose cost is your sole concern. Your decision process involves looking at a number of cars, ranking these cars in terms of cost from low to high, and picking the lowest-priced of the group.

But, with more than one objective, you ordinarily confront trade-offs among the objectives. One car may be the best in terms of your low-purchase-price objective, but a second is best in terms of appearance, yet a third provides the best warranty, and a fourth promises the lowest maintenance charges. In other words, in thinking about any one car versus the others, you are confronted with trade-offs; no one automobile ranks first in terms of every objective.

The situation for communities is no different. As a mayor, or city manager, or group of citizens attempts to make decisions involving the community's future, there are competing objectives present. Classic trade-offs always exist between highways and beauty, jobs and the quality of the natural environment, more social services and better ball diamonds, and so forth.

In general, we do a rather poor job of handling such situations. It's easy to get confused in thinking about various alternatives and the objectives you want to satisfy in purchasing an automobile. It's even more complex when other people's objectives are also involved, which is always the case in community decisions. Imagine trying to purchase an auto if you had to satisfy not only your own criteria, but also the objectives of three or a thousand other people.

It's at this point, the problem of dealing with multiple-objective decisions, that values and vision play important roles. Objectives are just another way of talking about values. For example, "having a beautiful community" is a value. So is "providing adequate care for the elderly." In fact, all objectives, one way or the other, reflect values. Even an objective such as "promote economic development in the community" is a value representing the judgment that ever-increasing incomes lead to an ever-increasing quality of life (an assumption I think is worth debating).

What happens in multiple-objective problems is that values are present but usually are not made explicit. In fact, the concrete objectives representing the values are not usually made very explicit.

But, one way or the other, the following takes place. There is a set of objectives floating around the table where people are making decisions. Moreover, these objectives are implicitly ranked in order of importance, and the objectives are weighted in relative importance to each other.

As an illustration, the city council of Algona, Iowa, voted to cut down approximately fifty mature oaks and maples lining the main street of that city in order to facilitate widening the street to four traffic lanes versus the existing two. Roughly twelve hundred people signed a petition to preserve the trees, but the city council, encouraged by the Iowa Department of Transportation and citing rather vague economic development motives, decided to remove the trees anyway.

The Algona City Council clearly ranked the objective of economic development higher than natural beauty. My personal values are such that I believe anytime you sacrifice trees to cement it is a bad decision. Obviously, the Algona council feels differently.

I am concerned at the moment, however, not with whose values are the best, but rather how communities go about thinking through problems where competing objectives are present. My personal experience tells me this is done badly in most cases. The objectives, let alone the values underlying the objectives, are seldom made explicit, and any sort of rational assessment of the various alternatives present relative to the stated objectives is absent.

As a first approach to this type of dilemma, a good place to start is a book by Charles Kepner and Benjamin Tregoe called *The New Rational Manager* (Kepner-Tregoe, Inc., 1981). The book contains some useful guidelines for handling multiple-objective decision problems in a democratic fashion. There are better, more sophisticated approaches to such problems, but the Kepner-Tregoe material is a good, basic way for communities to think through complex decisions where trade-offs are present. I have used such multiple-objective processes many times in my consulting, in my own managerial experience in seven years as a university dean, and in my personal life. They work very well.

At bottom, what defeats the effort to consciously manage change is *complexity*—the subtle and intricate connections among various elements in a problem. Things are a good deal more complex than we may realize. Suppose fifteen projects have been suggested for a community, and they must be prioritized. How many ways can this be done? There are approximately 1.3 trillion ways to rank fifteen things. No wonder even such an apparently simple task as setting budget priorities can lead to general confusion.

In designing a future for a community, in creating a vision, we are dealing with problems of enormous complexity. Everything seems to be related to everything else.

There is a way to handle this complexity, and it's called Interpretive Structural Modeling (ISM). ISM is a process for helping people to deal with the multitude of elements and interrelationships among the elements that always are present in attempting to synthesize a vision or a complex set of objectives of any kind. Thousands of applications of ISM have been carried out in such diverse fields as community planning, forestry management, university curriculum planning, and creating a vision for a corporation.

Last summer I did some work for a state department of housing and community development on the East Coast. The people in the department found themselves constantly overworked and seemed to be making no progress toward anything. After probing the department's seemingly innocuous mission statement with ISM, I discovered this department was, in fact, attempting to pursue sixty-four major and separate projects simultaneously. No wonder confusion and fatigue dominated.

ISM is a little too involved to explain clearly in this type of forum. But, if you are interested in ISM, take a look at John Warfield's *Societal Systems*. Warfield is the inventor of

ISM, and, be warned, his book is formidable. You can quite easily read around the difficult parts of the book, however, and get a good idea of what ISM is and does.

The idea, then, is to design a future for a community by creating vision, by using the major elements of that vision to supply criteria for community decision making, and to manage the complexity of the change process through several techniques like the ones suggested. In doing so, leaders will see progress, the community will move toward the mutual vision it has created, and traps will be avoided.

There is no magic in all of this, no need for great leaders or particularly charismatic people. Quite the opposite. I am talking about helping rather ordinary people to create extraordinary communities in which to live. The process of managing change, of getting from here to there while preserving those aspects of the present we find desirable and avoiding traps along the way, is do-able.

Hard work, supplemented by some solid techniques for managing change, such as those suggested, will get anyone through in fine style. And when yet another meeting has been completed, those attending it will find they have not only clearly moved one more step toward their vision, but also probably still like each other, as well. And that counts for something I think is rather important.

I Am Orange Band

The thought is a haunting one. It comes to me at odd times, unpredictable moments. I might be playing my guitar or reading or just driving along in the car. And suddenly I'm thinking about a fellow named Orange Band. I never met him, and I never will.

His name resulted from a small strip of plastic around his leg. I used to think he deserved a better handle. In Latin he was *Ammodramus nigrescens,* but that seemed too coldly scientific and species-like, in the same way I am *Homo sapiens.* What was needed, I thought, was a name that captured in a word or two his unique place in the scheme of things. Something that identified him as being the very last of his kind, that succinctly conveyed the isolation of his existence. A name that somehow reflected the infinite loneliness that must accompany a state of undiluted unity. For he was perfectly and unalterably alone.

But, in the end, I decided that Orange Band was a good name for him. He was plain, and he was gritty, and it suited him well. Besides, the simplicity of such a name is more than fitting if you are the only remaining dusky seaside sparrow and there is no one left to call it out. If I were the last of *Homo sapiens,* I think I would take such a name. And I would sit with my back against a granite ledge, near a river in a distant twilight colored blue, and say, "I am Orange Band," listening to the words come back to me through the trees and along the grass.

How do we measure loneliness? If the counting bears any relationship to the number of your species still around, then Orange Band was lonely. It had not always been so. The duskies were common once in the marshes of Merritt Island, Florida. They were six inches long, blackish above with a yellow patch near the eye, streaked in black and white lower down, and sang a buzzy song resembling that of a red-winged blackbird.

That was before we slowly pitched our faces skyward and murmured, "Space." Along with the mathematics of flight and the hardware to take us there, we had to deal with the nasty problem of mosquitoes that plagued the Kennedy Space Center. For reasons known only to people who conjure up such things, flooding the Merritt Island marshlands nearby seemed to be the answer to the mosquito problem. The water rose and took with it the nests of the dusky seaside sparrows.

There was one other place, just one, where the duskies lived. Propelled by conservationist pressures, the federal government lurched into action and spent something over $2 million to purchase 6,250 acres along the St. John's River. There were two thousand of the little songbirds living there. Ah, but highways came. Always the highways come. They come to bring more people who will need more highways that will bring more people who will need more highways. The marshes were drained for road construction and fire swept through the dry grass of the nesting grounds. Pesticides did the rest.

By 1979, only six dusky seaside sparrows could be found along the river. Five of them were captured. None were females. The last female had been sighted in 1975.

The *New York Times* duly noted the problem in the August 31, 1983, edition under a headline that read: "Five Sparrows, All Male, Sing for a Female to Save Species." And just below the *Times* article, in one of those ethereal juxtapositions that sometimes occur in newspaper layouts, was an advertisement for a chichi clothing store called Breakaway.

The copy above a photo of a smartly-turned-out woman went like this:

> You strive for spontaneity
> To take life as it comes
> The perfect complement to your dynamic lifestyle
> Our natural silver fox jacket
> Now during our Labor Day celebration
> Save $1000.00 off the original price
> Originally $3990.00, now $2990.00

In the swamps of Florida, spontaneity was on hold. So were dynamic lifestyles. The five male duskies were brought to Disney World's Discovery Island, were pensioned off and made comfortable. Orange Band was about eight years old.

So it was, not far from the place where we launch for other worlds, that a different kind of countdown began. By 1985, there were three of the little males left. Then one died in September of that year. On March 31, 1986, a second one died. That left Orange Band, by himself.

Now and then, I would think of Orange Band alone in his cage. The last member of the rarest species known to us. He became blind in one eye, became old for a sparrow, and yet he persisted, as if he knew his sole task was to sustain the bloodline as long as possible. I wondered if he wondered, if he felt sorrow, or excruciating panic at the thought of his oneness. Surely he felt loneliness. Charles Cook, curator of the zoo, issued periodic bulletins: "As far as we can tell, for a little bird like that he seems to be doing fine."

Still it was inevitable. On June 18, 1987, a *Washington Post* headline said: "Goodbye, Dusky Seaside Sparrow." Orange Band, blind in one eye, old and alone, was gone. He died by himself on June 17th, with no one, either human or bird, around.

But the day Orange Band died there was a faint sound out there in the universe. Hardly noticeable unless you were expecting it and listening. It was a small cry, the last one, that arched upward from a cage in Florida, ricocheted along galactic highways and skimmed past the scorched parts of an old moon rocket still in orbit. If you were listening closely, though, you could hear it . . . "I am zero."

Extinct. The sound of the word is like the single blow of a hammer on cold steel. And each day the hammer falls again as another species becomes extinct due to human activity. This is about 400 times the rate of natural extinction. Norman Meyers has projected that, by the end of this century, species will be vanishing at the rate of 100 per day.

In open defiance of the International Whaling Commission, Japan and Iceland continue to slaughter whales under the guise of "research." The real reason, however, is to supply the inexhaustible Japanese appetite for whale flesh. The great Calfornia condors are all in cages now. Less than twenty of the black-footed ferrets remain. The number of mountain gorillas has declined to under 450. The black duck is in serious trouble; nobody knows just how much trouble for sure. Over six million dolphins have been killed accidently by the Pacific tuna fleet the last thirty years. And have you noticed the decline of songbirds in Iowa?

The count rises, year after year. Roughly eleven hundred plants and animals are identified specifically on the endangered and threatened species list at the present time, but nobody really knows for sure how long the list should be. The reason is that science has not yet determined exactly how many species exist, and the job of identification is a long way from completion. With the clear-cutting of the tropical rain forests throughout the world, the numbers could be astronomical. For example, the current rate of forest loss is two hundred thousand square kilometers per year, and some estimates of species yet unknown in the tropical forests range as high as one million.

But we press on. With highways and toxic waste and

all-terrain vehicles and acid rain and pesticides and the straightening of pretty creeks to gain an extra acre or two on which to grow surplus crops. In the name of progress and something called "development," we press on, though we seem reluctant to define exactly what it is we seek. That definition, you see, likely is too frightening to contemplate, for the answer along our present course might be nothing other than "more."

More of what? Nothing in particular. Just more. We must have more, always more, for if we stopped, we would have less of that nothing in particular.

So the citizens buzz over blood and money around the boxing rings of Atlantic City and worry, ludicrously, about holding wineglasses properly and titter in a breathless way over Cher's ruthlessly salacious gown at the Academy Award ceremonies. And each day the hammer falls again. And each day another small cry arches upward; slowly and forever it arches upward. And sometimes I sit with my back against a granite ledge, near a river in a distant twilight colored blue, and say, "I am Orange Band," and the words come back alone through the trees and along the grass.

Democracy and the Natural Environment

Examples of environmental degradation are all around us now. The earth is warming due to human production and consumption activities. A deterioration in the ozone layer stemming from our use of chlorofluorocarbons is confirmed. The landfills bulge and nobody knows what to do with hazardous wastes. Our soil erodes from rapacious agricultural practices, acid rain is destroying prime forest land and water, and species extinction is accelerating at an alarming rate. There's more, but you get the point.

Meanwhile, the desire for and implementation of political freedom and, particularly, economic freedom are in ascendance nearly everywhere in the world. In Moscow, the comrades are running their own beauty parlors and auto repair shops and demanding ever more freedom of expression and the right to choose their own destinies. In Vietnam, the government is experimenting with the encouragement of privately owned small businesses in the retail and service sectors. Bulgaria is doing the same. Venture capital is supplied to local entrepreneurs in Hungary. Tanzania is cutting back on public payrolls, Angola is trying to sell state companies to private entrepreneurs, and Nigeria has abandoned exchange controls, while India witnesses the rise of a large middle class demanding less interference with its lives and businesses.

On the one hand, then, we should feel exuberance—freedom is afoot, unfettered commerce soars. At the same

---

This essay is from an address delivered at the Iowa State University Institute on World Affairs conference, "The Global Environment: Transforming the Ecological Crisis," November 10, 1989.

time, we are haunted by the not-so-vague sense that the very natural systems sustaining us are crumbling. Centrally planned economies are no better at dealing with the natural environment than are democracies. That much we know. But that's not the point here. The issue is this: Given the rising political and economic aspirations of much of the world, what can be said about the relationship between freedom and the treatment of nature?

There are, I think, three ideas central to all of this. The first has to do with the politics of democracy, particularly as democracy currently functions in America, for in one way or another, we are the model that others look to. Second, there is the matter of property rights. And, third, there is the ethic of economic growth, which, regardless of how you cast present trends in world economics, is the propellant for the increasing privatization we see just about everywhere.

Presumably, political freedom involves not only freedom of speech and other similar rights, but also the free election of a representative government. In the discussion of rights, our own Declaration of Independence posits: "That to secure these rights, Governments are instituted among Men, deriving their just powers from the consent of the governed." And from Lincoln, of course: "Government of the people, by the people, for the people. . . ." Furthermore, for good or for bad, we live with the legacy of Jeremy Bentham, who said: "The happiness of the individuals, of whom a community is composed, that is, their pleasures and their security, is the end and the sole end which the legislator ought to have in view."

In those words, and others like them, rests part of the dilemma we and the emerging democracies now confront in dealing with the natural environment and all other problems requiring sacrifice of the present for a long-run benefit.

The natural environment is slow to anger, so to speak. Like the quiet kid on the playground who endures years of abuse before exploding in rage, nature has been quiet and resilient, and, until the last few years when the effects of our abuse have become obvious, apparently suffered our mistreatment without complaint. Suddenly, or so it seems to many people, our water has gone bad, our soil has disappeared or been contaminated, and our air is fouled.

Were there warnings? According to Bill McKibben in a recent *New Yorker* article, a nineteenth-century Swedish scientist, Svante Arrhenius, recognized that humans were in the process of "evaporating our coal mines into the air." As early as a century before, Jean Baptiste-Fourier had speculated about this matter. The general scientific opinion, however, held that our oceans could absorb any excess carbon dioxide emissions. That rosy forecast was refuted in 1957 by researchers at the Scripps Institute of Oceanography.

Thomas Jefferson was an eloquent and ardent spokesman for soil conservation, recommending contour plowing, clover planting, and crop rotation to retain soil and soil fertility. And Hugh Hammond Bennett, the grand old man of soil conservation, was convinced of the dangers of soil erosion by 1903. He spent his life studying, writing, and speaking about the problem and published a U.S. Forest Service report, "Soil Erosion: A National Menace," in 1928.

There were others, many others, who warned us. Rachel Carson spoke of the dangers of chemicals in our biosystems thirty years ago. Nearly twenty years ago we celebrated Earth Day and promptly forgot about the Earth. In 1974, the first studies appeared warning of problems in the ozone layer. Worries about the clear-cutting of tropical rain forests have been around for years. But you don't need science, or even prophets. Anybody who has been looking at rivers and forests and birds knows what has been happening. We've been trashing the place.

Why? We consider ourselves God-fearing and prudent and forward-looking. We spend fifty-two cents of every tax dollar on military preparedness and threaten to wave lasers around outer space against those who might invade us. Given our fear of God and our potential enemies, how is that we have been able to ignore the destruction of our life-sustaining systems? If another country had poisoned our water, up their beaches we would have gone in force.

Some say that it's biblical, that certain convenient interpretations of scripture both allow and promote our dominance over the natural order. Others think it has to do with old habits stemming from the time when we confronted an unspoiled continent and, hence, saw no restrictions on exploiting resources and ridding ourselves of trash. I think it runs deeper than that. Besides, those explanations, which probably have some validity, don't promise much in the way of getting out of our current mess. Arguments about religion are unproductive, and, obviously, the limits of nature have been breached. I think it has to do with the liabilities of freedom and, more generally, the way we go about our daily business.

There is, I suggest, a rather natural, though not necessarily admirable, tendency to apply a high discount rate to the future. Given two alternatives, one that brings rewards in the short run but has great long-run costs, and another requiring present sacrifice but with possible long-range benefits of a substantial kind, it does not take much change in the discount rate as applied to flows of costs and benefits to make the short-term alternative dominant.

And, clearly, we manipulate, either overtly to suit our most pressing current needs or covertly, in a psychological sense, our discount rates to match our preferences for short-term gratification. In short, we apply high discount rates, rates of interest, to our decision making. And, as every student in basic finance knows, the short run always triumphs over the long run when that occurs.

This phenomenon is true even when we are dealing with

long-term tangible problems, such as decay of the physical infrastructure, that is, the repair of sewers, roads, water mains, and so forth. It is even more true when the short-term rewards are increases in tangible commodities versus more distant and intangible matters of beauty or wilderness or the survival of a species, including our own.

Alexander Hamilton, in the *Federalist Papers,* said: "Momentary passions and immediate interests have a more active and impervious control over human conduct than general or remote considerations of policy, utility, and justice." Carl Sagan took the metaphorical route: "We are like butterflies who flutter for a single day and think it is forever."

Why do we choose the short run and refuse sacrifice for benefits in the longer term? Are we evil? Ignorant or stupid? Surely not the former. Possibly the latter. Among other things, we lead busy lives. Consider the natural environment. Is it on your list of things to do today? For most people, probably not. It's not pressing, or so it seems. It doesn't fax you and ask for an immediate reply.

Connected with this is our system of learning that gets us by on a day-to-day basis. In simplistic terms, this system can be described as, "If it feels good, do it." Put another way, in light of the complexity we confront and the difficulty of detailed planning and decision making under such conditions of complexity, we respond to rewards and avoid punishments—overall, not a bad strategy for daily survival.

The problem arises when the long run must be taken into account. Sacrifice doesn't feel good; therefore, we don't want to do it, and we don't, most of the time. Who, then, should be taking care of the long run? Ideally, our elected officials are supposed to be those with the long view.

In the ideal, a workable democracy must always involve some compromise between what a strong elected representative believes is right and what his or her constituents say. But that's not the way it's working. In fact, politicians constantly are running for office. If the pronouncements of our Declaration of Independence and Lincoln and Bentham are to be taken seriously, this apparently is the way it should be.

But, we have been successful at transferring our short-run inclinations into our political preferences and demand that politicians accede to them. When it comes to matters requiring the government to ask us for self-sacrifice, we behave in much the same way that we do in our daily lives, favoring short-run rewards and avoiding punishments. And we transmit our feelings via the mails or lobbyists or campaign contributions or the ballot box.

The legendary columnist and political philosopher Walter Lippmann put it well:

> Faced with . . . choices between the hard and the soft, the normal propensity of democratic governments is to please the largest number of voters. The pressure of the electorate is normally for the soft side of the equations. That is why governments are unable to cope with reality when elected assemblies and mass opinions become decisive in the state, where there are not statesmen to resist the inclination of the voters and there are only politicians to excite and exploit them.
>
> . . . democratic politicians have preferred to shun foresight about troublesome changes to come, knowing that the massive veto (from the electorate) was latent, and that it would be expensive to them and their party if they provoked it.

Lippmann wrote that forty-five years ago. Things have not changed. No politician that I know of has yet said, "Citizens, the natural environment is in danger; you will be asked to sacrifice for the future good of us all." Even the power-holding conservatives are worried. Kevin Phillips, a conservative analyst, described the current state of things as a "frightening inability to define and debate America's emerging problems."

And President Bush's director of the budget, Richard

Darman, last summer blasted both the government and the voters for mimicking spoiled children with their demands of " 'now-nowism,' our collective short-sightedness, our obsession with the here and now, our reluctance adequately to address the future." A few months after Darman spoke, Bush joined with leaders from Britain, the Soviet Union, and Japan in blocking a sixty-eight-nation conference from adopting specific annual goals intended to cut carbon dioxide emissions by the major industrial countries.

In addition to short-term thinking, there is the problem of knowledge. In general, Americans have a distaste for the study of science, an even greater dislike for mathematics, and a complete misunderstanding of how knowledge is built. Add to this an intolerance for ambiguity, and you have the makings of ignorance and impatience with ecological science that must talk in terms of estimates and probabilities, at best. The problems confronting us are too new and too complex for quick and easy answers of the kind that both the electorate and politicians favor.

The cause-and-effect chains are long and subtle, with feedback effects and surprises present at nearly every stage. For example, the greenhouse effect may feed on itself once it gets under way. One possibility is that as carbon dioxide and other gases trap solar infrared radiation and the atmosphere warms, additional water vapor will be created, leading to further warming and even more water vapor. Or the warming may melt the permafrost, releasing methane contained within it, which in turn would lead to more warming.

It's all very subtle, all very complex, and apparently beyond our reach. An anecdote in *International Wildlife* illustrates this: A commuter in smog-choked Atlanta maneuvers an out-of-tune Chevrolet through backed-up rush hour traffic, and three years later trees die on a North Carolina mountaintop. At the moment, we know only three things:

1. There will be changes.
2. Some of these changes are going to be irreversible.
3. We are uncertain about the magnitude and timing of the changes.

As I said, Americans tend to be impatient with such uncertainties. In the absence of anything approaching conclusive proof, probabilities are necessary. Thinking about the future always involves probabilistic reasoning. But, it turns out, humans are not very good at estimating and using probabilities and tend to have a low tolerance for ambiguity overall. For example, there is plenty of evidence showing that humans assign higher-than-warranted probabilities to desirable outcomes and the reverse to unwanted outcomes.

This amounts to a kind of psychological denial. As Adlai Stevenson said: "Given the choice between disagreeable fact and agreeable fantasy, we will choose agreeable fantasy." And, I might add, when it comes to the natural environment, we deal with probabilities in a mighty curious fashion.

Here's an example. The Food and Drug Administration demands years of proof before a drug is released for human consumption. In other words, we ask for proof of safety. Yet, in terms of environmental impact, we forge ahead and environmentalists are asked to prove harm before questionable manufacturing or other practices are ceased. From a decision-making point of view, we employ a criterion of unwarranted optimism when it comes to nature and the reverse when it comes to drugs, even though both enter our biological systems.

In general, then, we favor the short term, while nature requires long-term thinking, and we most decidedly forward this preference to our elected officials or those seeking office. The fault, ultimately, is in the electorate and not in our public officials. I used to think it was the reverse, but eventually I came to understand that blaming politicians simply is a way of excusing ourselves. Another form of denial. In other words, we get the kind of leadership we deserve.

Eventually, in a democracy, events begin to outrun us. Though it's hard to imagine a United States without the Everglades, it now appears that they are dying, irreversibly so (and I am given to wonder at the *Ever* in Everglades). We see it happening, we don't want it to happen, but like the narcotics addict, every time we think about a cure, it seems worse than the disease, for it means short-run sacrifice for the long-run good.

Then there are the environmental problems of a worldwide nature, such as the greenhouse effect and the thinning of the ozone shield. Here we have something similar to what occurs within a democracy, in the sense that each nation is pursuing what it believes is good for itself. Each nation is independent, yet we seek to have all agree to ban, for example, chlorofluorocarbons or dirty coal burning processes, even when it is not in the short-term interests of any of them to do so.

Even the developed countries have been slow to act on these matters, and understandably so, for they are the major contributors to both of these problems. (The United States with about 5 percent of the world's population is responsible for approximately 25 percent of the world's commercial energy use each year.)

Now we ask the underdeveloped countries to come into line with us on restricting chlorofluorocarbon emissions and other such problems. Why should they? It's not in their interest to do so in the short term, and they have plenty of short-term problems to solve without cooperating in the solution of problems caused by those countries who have been so wanton in the use of the world's resources, countries that themselves are reluctant to change.

One of these short-range problems is poverty. Poverty is a major obstacle to intelligent treatment of the natural environment. The poor, with severely constrained sets of alternatives confronting them and criteria oriented to the short run even more than the rest of us, will surely not view environmental protection and enhancement as important criteria in making decisions. As a Jesuit priest from South America once told me: "You don't preach religion to people with empty bellies."

Or, as Thomas Fuller observed: "He that has nothing is frightened of nothing." And I might add, those who are hungry, poor, and thirsty care not about the condition of the river or acid in the rain, let alone the probabilistic forecasts about melting ice caps in the year 2050.

When you are poor, you get what you can today and to hell with tomorrow. As Indira Gandhi remarked, "Poverty is the biggest environmental problem in India."

So, along with the basic injustices, suffering, and human indignities that accompany poverty, we have a second-order effect in that deterioration of the very ecosystems that sustain us all will be encouraged, particularly as the developing nations attempt their long climb toward prosperity.

It's important to remember, for example, that 45 percent of Africa's population is under the age of fifteen. These people, understandably, want food and air conditioning and automobiles and the rest of what they see highly industrialized economies enjoying.

And the cycle starts to close. For as we now must devote more and more of our resources to crash programs for cleaning up the environment, undoubtedly the poor, those with the least political clout, will suffer as resources are transferred and reassigned to other priorities.

Private property rights seem to be a natural accompaniment to political and, certainly, to economic freedom. Rousseau, in "A Discourse on Political Economy" (1758), said: "It should be remembered that the foundation of the social contract is property; and its first condition, that every one should be maintained in the peaceful possession of what belongs to him."

Such rights bring us directly into the clash between private interest and the public good. I bluntly forecast that this clash, particularly in the realm of private property rights versus public rights, will become one of the major areas of debate in the next few decades.

Consider for a moment our rivers. They have been dammed and silted, polluted and drained, channeled and straightened, crossed by wire, and used as drag strips by the fools among us. During a long canoe trip through southern Minnesota and northern Iowa a few years ago, I encountered a small but clear example of what economists call *externalities,* which is, in essence, someone profiting by externalizing the costs of their operation onto someone else.

Along the northern part of the Shell Rock River, farmers have strung barbed wire across the river in the process of creating pasture for their cattle. Most of this wire carries electric current, some of it 110 volts. This is an externality. Not only are recreational opportunities spoiled, but also the cattle defecate in the water and destroy the riverbank and its soil- and water-retaining properties as they stomp around.

Yet, on April 6 of this year, the Iowa Senate Environment and Energy Committee killed a measure that would have required Iowa farmers to leave an uncultivated strip sixteen and a half feet wide between their fields and nearby rivers and streams. These are called *filter strips* and act as buffers to prevent erosion of our land and the poisoning of our waters by chemically laden soil. (I doubt that the width of such a filter strip is adequate, but it's certainly a beginning.)

As part of the debate over filter strips, Senator H. Kay Hedge, a Republican and farmer from Fremont said, "It bothers me that we'd set a precedent of being able to go in and remove privately owned land from production."

What the people who tout private property rights in matters such as these seem not to understand is that private property rights cease to carry any moral imperative when the behavior of those holding such rights are encroaching upon the rights of others—in this case the rights of the rest of us to enjoy unshackled streams, pure drinking water, and the assurance that a productive soil base remains in place for ourselves, the generations to come, and our fellow—nonhuman—members of the natural order.

Furthermore, it's important to note that the right of private property is a matter of culture, an artifact of civil society, not something ordained by the highest rational power in the universe. I see nowhere, by the granting of private property rights, have we also granted the right to despoil and plunder, to exercise what the distinguished English jurist Sir William Blackstone, in his *Commentaries on the Laws of England,* long ago called "the sole and despotic dominion" over the land and the resources of nature.

Lippmann also commented on this, using key phrases of Blackstone's as he wrote. He said:

> The ultimate title does not lie in the owner. The title is in "mankind," in The People as a corporate community. The rights of the individual in that patrimony are creations of the law, and have no other validity except as they are ordained by law. The purpose of laws which establish private property is not to satisfy the acquisitive and possessive instincts of the primitive man, but to promote "the grand ends of civil society"—which comprehend "the peace and security of individuals." Because the legal owner enjoys the use of a limited necessity belonging to all men, he cannot be sovereign lord of his possessions. He is not entitled to exercise his absolute and therefore arbitrary will. He owes duties that correspond with his rights. His ownership is a grant made by the laws to achieve not his private purposes, but the common social purpose. And, therefore, the laws of property may and should be judged, reviewed and, when necessary, amended, so as to define the specific system of rights and duties that will promote the ends of society.

This, then, is a doctrine of private property that denies the pretension to a "sole and despotic dominion." Historically, we saw a regression (in England) to a notion that property had only rights and no duties. Lippmann again: "Absolute private property inevitably produced intolerable evils. Absolute owners did grave damage to their neighbors and to their descendants: they ruined the fertility of the land, they exploited destructively the minerals under the surface, they burned and cut forests, they destroyed the wild life, they polluted streams. . . ."

So, the public philosophy, via Lippmann and Blackstone, can be stated as:

The Earth is the general property of all humankind and the creatures who share it with us.

Private titles of ownership are assigned by law-making authorities to promote the grand ends of civil society.

Private property is, therefore, a system of legal rights and duties—a product of culture rather than of divine origin.

If private property is a natural accoutrement to democracy, and it certainly seems to be, then democracies must immediately begin to lay bare the rights and privileges pertaining to such ownership. In spite of the farmer's wish to graze his cattle with access to the river and to plant his crops right up to the water's edge, I, as a member of the public, also have a powerful claim to float upon and to take my water from clean, unsilted waters, unhampered by barbed wire carrying 110 volts of current.

If you wonder why we flounder so in attempting to deal with our environmental problems, remember that politicians and the business community have, in general, disliked environmentalists.

Environmentalists represent, by speaking for nature, a cost of doing business, a cost that has heretofore not appeared on the income statements of businesses. Gross National Product (GNP), our much revered measure of social advancement, is computed through a sophisticated but severely flawed set of measurements called the *national income accounts.*

Unfortunately, these accounts do not measure the true cost of doing business nor of economic growth. For example, if a business firm produces a product and sells it, at some point the dollar volume of this product is counted in the GNP. But if, at the same time, this firm pollutes a river or the air, nowhere do these costs appear in our national income accounts, even though they are real and true costs of doing business.

If a business firm calculated its net profit before taxes by omitting, for example, the cost of its labor, we would argue that profit has been overstated. But in the destruction of our natural environment we have incurred costs that have not appeared in either our private or our national income accounts. Therefore, we consistently overstate our economic progress.

And our measurements can get unbelievably perverse. If we build a new sewage plant to clean up the river, this counts as a revenue in our national income accounts, not a cost, even though the plant was built to clean up the river that was fouled by firms and cities whose growth originally contributed to GNP, all the while fouling the river.

Business people know their prices do not reflect the true cost of doing business. So do politicians. Neither want to admit it, for such admissions cast considerable doubt on our progress as a society (as measured by economic growth), and if the true costs of production were assigned to a product, I suggest that many business firms would not be operating today. That's one reason, probably the major one, why the business community so stoutly resists environmentalists. Environmentalists argue for the inclusion of costs that heretofore have been ignored.

Recently, in Clinton, Iowa, an executive of a rendering firm operating under the name of National By-Products, in response to complaints about odors emanating from the plant, was quoted as saying to Clinton officials that the firm is "in the business to make money, not spend money." That attitude is exactly what I am talking about. The management of the rendering plant quite simply is stating, "We do not want to pay the true costs of our production activities."

Similarly, I doubt if Ronald Reagan would have been able to ask, "Are you better off now than you were four years ago?" with as much assurance if the true costs to the environment had been assigned to the production of the early 1980s.

Another reason environmentalists are not held in high esteem is that they are like little figures on the horizon jumping up and down holding signs that say "LIMITS." The encouraging words from Washington, and elsewhere in our political structure, are a result of no politican really wanting to tell the citizens of this country the truth. And the hard, grinding truth is this: We may not be able to continue to live the way we are now, because the natural environment cannot sustain our profligate ways.

Nobody, it seems, wants to break the bad news, for there is a tendency to shoot the messenger and forget about the fundamental underpinnings of our environmental dilemma. And the most critical underpinning is an economy and a society based on high-intensity consumption. Furthermore, increasingly it appears that our entire legitimacy as a society is based on such consumption.

We seek more economic consumption because we have been encouraged to seek more because more is good and less or the status quo is bad, according to the prevailing social philosophy of this country. Nobody, particularly the politician, wants to examine the legitimacy of our contemporary lives because the questions, let alone the answers, are troubling. As William Leiss puts it:

> The principle of legitimacy for modern society . . . now consists in a permanently rising level of consumption. . . . There is no apparent end to the escalation of demand and no assurance that a sense of contentment or well-being will be found in the higher reaches of material abundance. . . . In those societies where such a market economy already exists or is in the process of formation, a principal article of faith is that the economy should continue to expand and to offer an ever-widening array of commodities for consumers. And a principal concern for such societies is to ensure that sufficient quantity of energy and material resources will be available for this purpose.

That is frightening, truly frightening, and truly sad. And I believe Leiss is right.

Moreover, what becomes even more frightening is that resource availability may not be the most pressing problem in the near term. It likely will be disposal of the by-products of our production and consumption, of our use of those resources. For example, consider the carbon dioxide emissions causing approximately 50 percent of the greenhouse effect.

In a recent issue of *Sierra* magazine, James Udall stated:

> "Global warming is that familiar nemesis, the energy crisis, recurring in a new guise. For decades the prevailing assumption has been that a fossil-fuel-based economy would be constrained by oil, gas, and coal depletion. . . . But global warming has turned that paradigm on its head: It now appears that the atmosphere's ability to assimilate fossil-fuel wastes will be the limiting factor. The question is no longer how much oil, gas, and coal we have, but how much we can afford to burn.

And, as other countries attempt to emulate our wasteful practices, the situation is going to become even more critical than it is now, and it's already critical. One illustration is

China. To power its development program, China plans to nearly double coal consumption in the next decade. By 2025 it may be the world's largest emitter of carbon dioxide, and China apparently cares little about what the rest of us think.

The impacts stemming from the high-intensity-consumption society are everywhere. I listed a number of them earlier. More than that, I firmly believe that consumption exceeding all reasonable bounds has led to what I call a dopey culture, a culture that actually gets excited about new car models, the current range of intellectual garbage offered on commercial television, the latest stereo innovation, the latest facial cream, and a new design of toothpaste tube. It has all become mindless.

The "Born to Shop" nonsense reached its zenith, or perhaps its nadir, recently in the form of one of those pseudo–talk shows, which really are nothing more than marketing ploys, where the audience actually—this is true—was breaking into applause at the demonstrated performance of a car wax. I didn't stay with the program long enough to discover if a standing ovation along with cries of "Bravo!" was given at the end. Probably.

And, in this mindlessness, in this constant need for shallow and transitory stimulation, we have forgotten how to think and, therefore, we have lost the capacity to deal with the issues of a democratic society in an enlightened and civilized fashion. Thus, we cry to our scientists for yet another technological fix, instead of examining ourselves and confronting the terrifying fact that we might just have to change our own behavior.

The electorate, as a whole, apparently doesn't want to change, and politicians don't want to change because the electorate doesn't. To change means uncertainty, ambiguity, and a confrontation with the nasty question of how we slice up the pie if the pie is not growing or is growing at a slower rate.

We Americans are approaching 250 million in population. What about the rest of the world, the other five billion? You needn't have taken advanced mathematics to compute that not everyone can live as we do, and that will lead you to conclude that *we* cannot continue to live as we do.

Though we should endlessly applaud the world trend toward more open societies, toward freedom, toward a free press and democratic principles, our applause should be muted in light of the problems that accompany freedom. And almost as if they are two separate streams of events, though apparently interlocked in some subtle fashion, the drive for political freedom is being accompanied by experiments in economics designed to foster, regardless of the name given it, economic growth.

Democracy brings no assurance that the critical problems of our time, particularly the problems of the natural systems that sustain us, will be dealt with intelligently or with dispatch. An enlightened dictatorship, though I certainly do not favor the form of rule, is probably more capable of handling many of our problems than we can as a free and democratic people, as we struggle with a short-sighted electorate, politicians rather than statesmen, the philosophical issues of private property, and the idea that rapacious economic growth is the very foundation of the legitimacy of our society.

And that's what really causes me concern. If we cannot come to grips with the problems that democracy has fostered, then the problems themselves—though this can be viewed as overly pessimistic—may bring about the decline of democracy. And all the debate, all the tears, the millions who have died to protect democracy from external threats, all of this will have been in vain, for we will have allowed our own inadequacies to destroy ourselves.

Sustainability is the first problem of any society. Nothing, not even the advances of foreign powers, can threaten a nation more than the demise of the natural systems underpinning its sustainability. If we allow the continued deterioration of our environment, I can see one or more possible scenarios where our own general freedoms will be abridged in an effort to confront the problems of resource use and disposal of discommodities.

Arnold Toynbee was brutal in his assessment of the fragility of freedom:

> Man is a social animal; mankind cannot survive in anarchy; and if democracy fails to provide stability, it will assuredly be replaced by some socially stabilizing regime, however uncongenial this alternative regime may be. A community that has purchased freedom at the cost of losing stability will find itself constrained to re-purchase stability at the price of sacrificing its freedom. This happened in the Greco-Roman world; it could happen in our world too if we were to continue to fail to make democratic institutions work. Freedom is expendable; stability is indispensable.

We tend to accept democracy as if it were the norm rather than the exception in the conduct of human affairs. On the contrary, freedom is the exception rather than the rule and is a rather recent development at that. And, as an early French philosopher said: "Freedom is the luxury of self-discipline." That luxury, like other exotic and rare commodities, currently is in exceedingly short supply. Somebody is going to impose discipline on us; there is no other choice.

I prefer that we begin to run against the traditional human grain, to forgo short-term behavior and think of the natural systems that sustain us and the creatures besides ourselves that inhabit those systems, before the solutions to our problems become more draconian than they already promise to be. I am not optimistic that, given our current ways of behaving, we will make the necessary adaptations.

We stand here confronted by one of the most profound transition periods in human history. Resources obviously are limited, while the by-products of our use of these scarce resources are poisoning our environment, resulting in even scarcer resources in the form of clean air, pure water, and fertile soil. At the same time, population explodes in the poorer countries, and these countries demand their own rights to the pleasures they see us enjoying, let alone the minimum necessities, which implies even more economic growth on a planet already staggering from the load we are placing upon it. Clearly, we cannot follow the same path we have been following. Clearly, we will be asked to change.

Two Encounters in the West

WESTERN NEW MEXICO, HIGH DESERT—If I were into rear-window signs on automobiles, which I'm not, mine would read, "Photographer on board; I brake for sunsets." So I'm off the pavement and onto the red dirt shoulder as rich lavender blankets a mesa in late afternoon. Pitching from the car with tripod and bag, I run to a small rise and start setting up. A battered pickup stops thirty yards in front of me. In jeans and wide-brimmed hat, an old Indian man gets out to . . . ah . . . relieve himself. Unabashed, he is, and in plain view, until he sees the camera. With only a slight lurch toward modesty, he turns and partially hides himself behind the open truck door.

Not completely, though. The big lens easily can shatter his flimsy attempt at privacy. For a moment, just a brief one, I am tempted. A slight movement left along the horizontal axis of the tripod is all it will take; a vertical shot will capture both the mesa and the man. Old truck, old man, old country, old physical needs. Everything is there. A classic shot composes itself.

It's the kind of photograph certain critics love, preferably executed in grainy black and white. I can visualize it hanging in the Metropolitan Museum, a personal retrospective. Sunday afternoon, unpretentious wine and Brie, and the sagacious nodding of heads as connoisseurs examine a print entitled, "New Mexico Indian Piddling beside Truck at Sunset." My reputation forever could ride on that one shot.

He buttons up, glances over his shoulder toward me and waves. I wave back, then focus on the mesa. But good light has already moved on, running hard before a storm front. The chance has flickered past me, gone to that place where lost images rest and laugh about their escapes. I load the equipment into the car, wondering where the next town lies, remembering that old men understand one another. They have come to terms with the unfading trade-offs between fame and conscience and seek only peace and dignity in desert twilights. To hell with the critics.

BIG SUR, CALIFORNIA—In knee-high rubber boots and mountain parka, I have come to this beach at dawn and alone. Sunrise struggles unsuccessfully with the mountains at my back as I leave a grove of twisted cypress and move onto the sand, following a creek cutting its way to the Pacific. Watching the sea rocks for the first sign of good light, I almost miss a curious trace in the sand at my feet. The track is about three feet wide and smooth, with gouges on either side of it at even intervals.

Hunkering down, I touch the marks, as if they can speak of what created them. Except for the breakers on the shore, there is silence. I let my eyes follow the track toward the sea. Something large and brown is at the end of this strange path. Something large and brown and moving.

The first camera out of my knapsack is loaded with slow film from the previous evening's work. The second, containing faster film, has four exposures left. I mount that one on my tripod and sling the other around my neck, moving forward as I work. Carefully I go. This is not my territory; I'm not familiar with the wildlife of either the forest or the water in this place. I ford the creek, circling, trying to get in front of whatever it is ahead of me.

Now I can see the face. Mounted on a body that weighs several thousand pounds, it's a strange, sad face, with brown eyes resembling smooth beach stones and a trunklike proboscis. Using its flippers, the animal heaves itself nearer the Pacific. It has seen me and raises its head for a better view, then lowers it again and lies upon the sand in the way my dog lies upon a carpet, chin down, watching me, blinking.

From twenty feet, the brown eyes show clearly in the 200-mm glass. They are looking directly at me. I think the look is fear or at least a wary curiosity. I begin to sort through the feelings I have about disrupting the lives of other living things with my intrusions, and, clearly, I have intruded upon a peaceful moment that could have done without me.

I flog my memory for the images in all the wildlife manuals I have read. What is this? I should know. Not a sea lion. Wrong nose, too big. Not a walrus, though in size and behavior it has that look. Though I am not passionate about remembering the names of things and, in fact, believe that sometimes we are too intent on labeling the world about us, I should know what this creature is called.

The animal is placed wrong for a good shot. Low on the sand, rocks of the same color immediately to its back. No matter. I am content just to shoot a couple of frames for the record and let it be. Then I remember. The creature is an elephant seal, fairly rare at one time, but lately seen more often along these coasts. It has spent the night far up on the beach and, like the dawn, struggles now to find the water.

Six-foot waves hammer old rocks as the seal lunges its way into the creek, stopping now and then to look at me. The water deepens where the creek meets the ocean, and the animal's awkwardness begins to disappear. On land it was a huge lump of mud, flopping and squishing its way across the sand. In the water, it is something quite different. Sleek and fast, sliding deep, disappearing in a moment through a narrow channel between two large rocks.

Sunrise finds a crack in the mountains and turns the beach faded rose. A three-foot trace remains in the sand, with flipper marks on either side, leading toward the Pacific.

I reload a camera, looking for good light on the seascape. But I am thinking yet about the brown eyes of *Mirounga angustirostris* as it looked at me, flogging its memory and its manuals, recognizing me finally, and then rolling through the foam into deep water. Gone.

The Forums We Choose

I'll get right to it: The problems we confront dwarf the forums we institute to deal with the problems. Consider first the typical newspaper column running 750 to 800 words. Keeping your thoughts within those boundaries and saying anything at all, I'll admit, is an art form, a tough one to master. And I respect those who can do it consistently and well. But that's not enough space to explain, comment upon, and offer solutions to any truly significant problem. The virtues of brevity, here, are overwhelmed by the "undermodeling" of the problem being discussed.

Then there are the presidential debates. Brief questions, brief answers, brief rebuttals, and two-minute summaries. At the conclusion, I ask myself: "What is this candidate's world view? How does all of this fit together?" The answer is always the same: I don't know.

So the president is elected and holds periodic meetings with the press. White House reporter: "Mr. President, what is your position on carbon dioxide emissions and the impact on economic growth in the West that might come from restricting such emissions?"

President: "I'm glad you asked that. First, we must examine the history of the human idea of progress and its relationship to the growth ethic. Then I'll turn to the question of the role growth plays within developed countries and the danger to our economy of restricting emissions. Following that, I'll discuss the potential feedback effects, both economic and ecological, resulting from carbon dioxide emissions all over the world, particularly with regard to impacts on world hunger and the exacerbating matter of population growth. Then. . . ."

Obviously, that's not what the reporter wants, and that's not what the president is prepared to offer. In order to escape saying little about much, the president says nothing at all. Besides, the president doesn't know the answer to the question, and the reporter probably wouldn't understand it if he did, since mastery of about seven disciplines is necessary to handle the conceptual difficulties involved.

And please don't tell me that television talk shows, such as "Crossfire," do anything more than provide entertainment and income for the good ol' analysts from our nation's capital who participate. Next time you watch one of these programs, ask yourself at the end of it: "What is the output of all of this; what do I know now that I didn't know at the beginning?" The answer most of the time is "nothing." The results from various "Meet the Press"–type programs are the same. The format and time constraints do not allow meaningful exploration of complex problems. A question here, an answer there. None of it fits together; none of it makes any sense.

Maybe books are the answer. In a way they are, but candidates usually don't write books on anything, let alone their syntheses of pressing problems. Moreover, a relatively small proportion of the electorate reads serious books, and even if it did, rapidly evolving problems can make books obsolete in short order.

The magazines. How about those? There are some that tackle serious issues and allow the necessary space for the problem to be dealt with. For example, the *New Yorker* consistently prints long synopses of forthcoming books. Recently, a book by Bill McKibben, *The End of Nature,* was featured. The first part of the article dealt with the warming of the earth, requiring an understanding of how approximately thirty elements all interact with one another to cause the effect, and McKibben's was an attenuated explanation. It took me about five hours to get through the piece, including note-taking, reflection, and the construction of a quasi-mathematical model tracing the cause-and-effect relationships he was exploring. All of this work was necessary to understand the author's argument. So I'll admit that some magazines do provide a reasonable forum, yet the discussions tend to be couched, almost always, in everyday language, and this language is not powerful enough for conceptualizing truly complex problems. The same is true of most books written for general audiences.

My least-favorite forum is the public hearing on, for example, highway projects. At the front of the room is a phalanx of experts who have spent months studying the problem. Matched against them are concerned citizens who are not experts and who are allowed, by the announced rules of the meeting, sixty seconds to offer their observations. The result is technical demagoguery at its worst by the assembled experts who already know what they are going to do before the meeting commences. "Thank you for your comments, Good Citizens," they say, sweeping up their twelve volumes of studies and smiling surreptitiously at one another.

The outcome of our choice of forums is this: We either treat serious issues superficially or we choose issues that fit our forums. Do I have any suggestions? Yes, I do. But this essay already is over eight hundred words. So I'll write another one that extends my argument, by which time you'll have forgotten what my original point was.

Brokerage

Stanley Walk and Allen Kruger, proprietors of the Sportsman's Lounge and related enterprises in St. Ansgar, go unbounded. They subscribe not to limits and are unmoved by small-town demands for convention. Moreover, even in our darker times, they believe in Iowa and have little patience with those who feel otherwise. So, to them, it seemed perfectly natural to have an autograph party at the tavern to celebrate the publication of a new book dealing with Iowa.

Now, those of delicate, patrician tastes might see contradictions, or at least curious impropriety, in this idea—books and taverns and all. Not Stanley Walk, not Allen Kruger. "Get the author to commit, and we'll handle the rest," they said to the Iowa State University Press. "All right, let's do it," the author replied. Up went the flyers in the grocery stores of Worth and Mitchell counties. Arrange a radio interview on one of the local stations with the author. Get announcements on television and in the papers. Post signs, talk about it, plan and promote.

The weather turned rough in early November. Snow squalls throughout the day of the signing. Cold, and windy, and wet. The boys playing cards at the big circular table in the back never did figure out what was going on. By ten in the morning, there were piles of new books in plastic shrinkwrap stacked on a table. Some guy with long, gray hair—probably a liberal, the card players guessed—showed up with a pen and started signing copies of the book for people from such alien civilizations as Osage, Mason City, Fort Dodge, smaller Iowa towns, and southern Minnesota.

At lunch, a choice of beef or chicken, the author read an essay from the book to forty people who had paid $7.50 to eat and listen. One of them, a veterinarian, said, "It was a religious experience." The author's mother sat at the head table and recognized all the people in the story, herself included.

By afternoon, on a Saturday in early winter, it was a tableau straight out of everybody's vision of how America ought to be. Part Norman Rockwell, part Thomas Jefferson. In booths along the wall and tables down the middle, people were sitting quietly, drinking coffee or sipping a beer, reading the book.

For some reason, a number of political figures, elected and otherwise, had shown up. Their presence resulted in a kinetic discussion of what those folks like to call "issues," along with an impromptu strategy session for last-minute campaigning. Proponents of keeping Brushy Creek just the way it is, in the face of threats to build a dam in the wilderness area, arrived, commandeered a booth, and argued their cause to all who would listen. Next to them, other folks were planning a conference on rivers. The author signed more books, and the boys playing cards at the big circular table in the back were getting even more confused, swiveling around between hands just to keep track of things.

Among the guests was the author's high school typing teacher. While signing her book, he reflected that she probably had as much to do with getting the book finished as anyone else. An Osage man claimed that he and several other hunters had sworn off of goose hunting after reading one of the author's polemics on the subject. Upon hearing that, the author offered to print "Civilized Adult" across the man's forehead, but that was judged to be unwise, somewhat overdone.

KGLO television, from Mason City, clanked in with cameras and cords, requesting an interview with the author.

The man with the questions wanted to talk about economic development and computers; the author wanted to talk about shooting pool and rivers.

Snow blew down the main street of St. Ansgar as a fortyish woman with silver hair and a nice smile purchased a book and covertly inquired, "How can I get you to read the rest of the book to me?" The author replied, "Just ask, I'm easy." Mike, whose last name disappeared along with a scrap of paper, wants to show the author secret places along the Cedar River. Great. Spring will be perfect for that.

Stanley Walk beamed, served the customers, and carried more books from his office to the signing table. Allen Kruger argued politics. Stanley and the author talked about a poetry reading at the tavern, with maybe some music to go along with it. Sounds good. It'll get done sometime. By 3:30, the demand for literary sustenance was tapering off. The author packed up his pen, and his mother, and drove south along blacktop roads, while the politicos stayed behind to discuss issues and, in Shakespeare's words, figure out how to "circumvent God."

Stanley calls with the tally. Ninety-six books were sold that day. That's nice, but slightly irrelevant, not what's important here. The point is there are people out there who write or play music or do theater or create visual beauty or have problems to discuss. And there are people out there who want to read the words or listen to the music or see things of beauty or participate in the solving of nasty dilemmas. The predicament is one of brokerage, of getting all those folks together.

It can be done. Stanley Walk and Allen Kruger did it, and life became a little richer for everyone concerned because of it. The ideal of a literate, caring, sensitive, and participative society is attainable, at least in Iowa. All that's required is a little brokerage. We proved that on a snowy November day in St. Ansgar.

One Day...on a Beach...in California

What the beginners who ask me about photography don't understand are patience, preparation, and perseverance, waiting for the light and being ready when it comes. I had been three weeks on the road, shooting my way through south Texas, then New Mexico and Arizona. The winter light had been thin and dry, not good, and I was working hard, straining for every bit of interesting sun, studying mesas at twilight and the desert floor at dawn.

Sometimes, I think it's not the fault of nature, but rather my own. Sometimes I just see better. But, for whatever reason, the light was not there when I was there. I had the feeling it was just behind me or just in front of me.

It came once, that wonderfully soft, filtered, post-thunderstorm yellow in late afternoon, west of Albuquerque. But I was on I-40 and couldn't find an exit that allowed me what I wanted. Then it was gone, the light was, in fifteen minutes.

But I stood my ground, and waited, kept the lenses clean, and looked. Finally, in Big Sur, in January, it came. The night before, I had read my poetry in front of a stone fireplace at the River Inn. Maybe that did it.

At dawn, the little creek flowing through colored sand looked like raindrops sliding down the neck of a blue heron. The 24-mm stretched the sand and creek and got me what I wanted, while someone slept in a tent only twenty yards away. Then sunlight found a crack in the mountains at my back and turned the beach into bands of color. A half-hour later I watched the waves, saw a fine one coming with the sunlight running down its spine as it passed rocks jutting into the water. I got that, too, with my 200-mm.

Late in the day, there were others on the beach with cameras. But the wind came up, hard and cold, and they retreated to their cars before sunset. Sunlight switched to overcast and back again, though when you've watched enough sunsets, stood looking out to sea enough times as darkness runs toward you, the probabilities can be calculated. And, this time, they pointed toward a spectacular sunset.

A man went by, camera around his neck, light clothing. He had come to California where it's warm in the winter, so they say. "Ya think it's going to be a good sunset?" he shouted over the wind and surf. I nodded, standing beside my tripod, watching the tide run up toward my camera bag on the sand.

"Boy, I'm sure cold! You're dressed for it," he continued, looking at me. I nodded again, warm inside my long underwear, wool shirt and sweater, navy watch cap, and mountain parka. He left.

And, riding hard on winter surf and winter wind, the sunset came, wild and red and striped, just as I guessed it would be. I was alone on the beach, while the others who had been there sipped cocktails and stared at menus in a woodland restaurant, cursing the cold and the wind, their camera bags underneath the table.

What to Do about Brushy Creek

My phone rings. The man on the wire is outraged at the controversial proposal to build a lake in the Brushy Creek State Recreation Area. He wants me to tour the area with him, to what end I'm not sure. In any case, he's mad as hell, understandably, over the destruction of wildlife habitat and loss of scenic values that will accompany the lake.

In my mail, a few days later, is a long and passionate document written by a fisherman who, with equal logic on his side, believes the proposed lake is a sound idea. On the other hand, my local environmentalist friends are opposed to the lake. But economic development leaders in the Fort Dodge area believe the lake is desirable.

This month (September 1988), in an effort to influence legislation on the project, those who support the preservation of Brushy Creek in its present state are inviting lawmakers to tour the area. A bill to spend $5.6 million on the construction of the lake will come before the General Assembly next year. Already, the Iowa Department of Natural Resources has authorized the expenditure of $200,000 to study the lake's design.

The struggle over Brushy Creek is a divisive and curious battle that has been in the works for a long time. In a state that ranks at the bottom in the amount of public lands available, those of us who believe in more open spaces ought to be fighting for the expansion of such space and against the common enemies of mindless development and destructive agricultural practices rather than among ourselves. That's why it's curious.

Moreover, this nasty confrontation probably is unnecessary. The whole state of affairs surrounding Brushy Creek fairly reeks of bad public management coupled with a lack of creativity. What is needed here is something I like to call an *expansion of the choice set.*

For various reasons, humans have a tendency to place artificial constraints on their range of choices. The Brushy Creek conflict is, I suggest, a situation where the range of alternatives has been unduly constrained.

Let's do the following: Find another ravine containing water flow in the same general location that will provide a lake of equal or greater size. Now, first of all, supporters of the present lake proposal are going to tell me that's not possible. Maybe they're right, but I doubt it. Perhaps building the lake on land already controlled by the state seems simpler and maybe a half-million or so dollars cheaper to some planners than acquiring private lands for the project.

Okay, it might cost a little more. What's the cost-benefit ratio look like on the Brushy Creek lake compared with the same numbers for another location? In less time than it takes to say "hikers and horses," someone will conjure up some apparently unbeatable numbers favoring the selection of Brushy Creek as the lake site. These numbers will be flawed, value-laden, and partly grounded in midwestern stubborn.

Obviously, new land will have to be acquired. How much land and how much money? Six hundred acres? A half-million dollars? Three-quarters of a million dollars? What's the loss in productive agricultural land? Not much. Terrain appropriate for a lake is pretty marginal for any farm use. Besides, we seem unconcerned about the loss of farmland when it comes to pouring cement over it for highways or shopping centers.

What are the benefits of an alternate site? Plenty. Start computing the loss of unique wildlife habitat, trees, riding and hiking trails, campers, and so forth in Brushy Creek.

Those numbers count as benefits for an alternative location. Roll that into the cost-benefit equations and see what it looks like. I'll bet the result is surprising. Then toss in the nonquantifiable judgments about scenery, solitude, and similar things usually forgotten in cost-benefit measurements. Stir this all together, and see what happens.

Beyond the relative merits of various locations for the lake, it's the political and social elements of this problem that concern me as much as anything. There are cogent arguments on both sides of this issue. Good arguments for the lake, equally good arguments for the preservation of Brushy Creek as it exists now. This state needs to be unified in its efforts for conservation and open spaces, not divided, and I hate to see Iowans fighting Iowans over a situation that probably can be resolved with some creativity and hard thought.

There is a chance here for the Department of Natural Resources (DNR) to demonstrate real organizational maturity. Once an organization has put the full weight of its managerial egos on the line for a specific alternative in a decision-making situation, it's very difficult to back off and take another long, hard, open-minded look.

From personal experience as a manager and from my consulting, I know just how tough that is. I also know that the ability to do exactly that is the mark not only of a creative mind, but also is conclusive evidence of mature people and of an effective, well-managed organization.

In addition, the DNR already has put considerable effort into the Brushy Creek site. They will experience what I label the "sunk-cost drag," which is a reluctance to change course based on past costs, both direct and indirect, psychic and financial. It's a rather natural and normal proclivity. But it's not a very productive one in most cases. I think the Brushy Creek project is one of those circumstances.

In fact, all parties to this affair need to exhibit some maturity in the form of cooperation. The DNR wants a lake.

So do fisherfolks and boaters. The same is true for the economic development people in the Fort Dodge area and probably some lawmakers.

Those who want Brushy Creek preserved in its present condition should start wanting a lake as much as those already in favor of it. That includes environmentalists, the horse folks, birdwatchers, hikers, wildlife enthusiasts, and all sorts of other people. They should join forces with the prolake people to find another location and funding for the lake.

Now, let's see what kind of a lobbying force this represents if everybody gets on the same side. Here's my count, and it's probably incomplete: lawmakers in favor of a lake, lawmakers who want Brushy Creek preserved in its present form, lawmakers who want to avoid a political slaughterhouse in the next General Assembly, the entire equestrian industry in Iowa and supporters elsewhere, environmentalists of every stripe, economic development officials from Fort Dodge and surrounding areas, the DNR, boaters, fisherpeople, swimmers, picnickers, hikers, water-skiers, and anyone else with enough common sense to recognize that the present set of alternatives simply is not rich enough. I suggest that's plenty of clout, if it is unified, to get a non–Brushy Creek lake for that part of the state. Furthermore, there is a good deal of uncertainty in the present situation for each side. The politics of the matter are such that a lake may or may not be built. There will be winners and losers, substantial joy and incredible sorrow mixed with anger. This all can be changed to a situation where the probability is close to 1.0 for happiness on all sides.

Currently, there are only two alternatives under consideration: build the lake at Brushy Creek; don't build the lake at Brushy Creek. That's why there's conflict.

The problem needs to be recast so it appears as follows: Build a lake in the Fort Dodge area at site A, or build a lake in the Fort Dodge area at site B, or build a lake in the Fort

Dodge area at site C, and so forth. If sites A, B, C, and others like them are non–Brushy Creek sites, considerable political pressure can be generated by the joint efforts of pro-lakers and the Brushy Creek preservation folks.

Still, I can almost hear the whines and groans out there from those who believe no other site is possible. I've seen how much destruction earth-moving machines can do to woodlands in an hour. Those same beasts can also rearrange a site that's not quite perfect, yet, for a lake. It can be done, if we're creative enough.

The Committee for the Preservation of the Brushy Creek Valley and other anti-lake forces should immediately meet with development officials and other pro-lakers to form the Committee for a Lake in the Fort Dodge Area. Better yet, form a Committee for Environmental and Economic Development in the Fort Dodge area and make it a permanent group. The push for a better solution to this problem can then begin with the assistance of key lawmakers who, I'm sure, do not relish the bitter and destructive fight that will accompany this piece of legislation.

Get some organization, manage the effort well, and start looking for an alternate site where a lake can be built, pronto. If a small percentage of the effort and money that's being expended in the present battle is spent on finding a creative alternative, the alternative will be found, the lake will be built in short order, Brushy Creek will be preserved.

Most of all, this is a chance for the DNR to exert strong, positive leadership in the state. There has been criticism of the department for being unresponsive to citizen input and for being somewhat high-handed in its undertakings. The smart money within the DNR, or other areas of state government if the DNR is too lethargic or too stubborn, will see this as an opportunity to pull off one of the great managerial and public relations coups of the last few decades in Iowa.

Frankly, I'm appalled that our public officials, who profess such great interest in attracting tourists and new business to our state, have let this desire for a lake evolve into the current, dismal mess. The situation, as it stands, is laissez-faire at its very worst. Good managers know when to stay out of situations and when some guidance and conflict resolution are needed. They are needed here.

If the horse riders help the economic development people to help the tourism promoters to help the water enthusiasts to help the environmentalists, we'll all get what we want. At the moment we have a a win-lose state of affairs that needs to be converted to a win-win situation. Think of the boundless euphoria on both sides that will emerge when construction of a fine lake on a non–Brushy Creek site is approved. This will be a victory for rationality, creativity, and cooperation, and it should be endlessly celebrated. Keep that image in mind.

It can be done. The present course is not only needlessly adversarial and damaging to the interlocked objectives of recreation, tourism, economic development, and the expansion of public lands in Iowa—it also is silly. A better way can be found. If the state won't do it, the citizens should. Then, in the next election, we should put people in office who have the guts, sensitivity, and intelligence to deal with such eminently manageable situations as Brushy Creek.

Nature, Decision Making, and the Tasks before Us

The word *hubris* is of Greek origin and means "overbearing pride." It means "presumption, arrogance." And hubris describes accurately the human attitude and human behavior toward the natural systems sustaining us. Though we are part of nature, and always have been, oddly enough we do not see things that way.

Somehow, we have come to view nature as "out there," as something apart from us, as a source for raw materials and recreation and as a sink for the undesirable remnants of our production and consumption processes. This outlook has not always been with us. Early peoples saw themselves as tightly interlocked with nature and formed mystical bonds with the natural order. It's easy to understand why.

Clearly, if daily survival depends upon the movements of game or the largesse of fruit on the trees and berries on the bush, if a hard winter means death and a warm summer brings good traveling, then it becomes normal to feel part of nature rather than above it.

For all of this reverence, though, many ancient civilizations made the same mistakes we have made and are making. For example, the Mycenaean culture, which flourished on the Aegean islands and coasts in the second millennium before Christ, adopted the Greek concept of Gaea, the Earth

---

This essay was the keynote address delivered at the Governor's Conference on Environmental Education, Springbrook State Park, Guthrie Center, Iowa, January 12, 1990.

Mother, and continued the celebration and worship of Gaea that was part of Greek culture. Yet they wantonly cut forests for export and for trivial uses of their own and even turned to burning as a way of opening more areas for their flocks. The naked hills were not replanted, and the soils washed away in the rains. Plato wrote about this rapacious use of the land eight hundred years later and said: "What now remains compared with what then existed is like the skeleton of a sick man, all the fat and soft earth having been wasted away, and only the bare framework of the land being left."

There are other illustrations. As sixteenth-century Spanish explorers landed in what we call the Los Angeles basin, they noted the smoke from Indian campfires hanging in the air, trapped by what is now known as the inversion layer. In the first century B.C., the drinking waters of Rome were being polluted. Recent evidence suggests that the advanced Mayan civilization, which had reached a population of five million by A.D. 900, collapsed because of soil erosion.

And the great societies of Mesopotamia apparently succumbed not to invasion, as we all learned in the fifth grade, but rather to cumulative environmental stress, which undermined their economies and eventually reduced food supplies. In this case, it appears that irrigation without proper drainage was the cause, which resulted in a waterlogging and salinization of the soil. Other examples can be found in Guatemala, and in North Africa, which once was the granary of the Roman Empire; now Libya and Algeria import half of their grain.

So, contrary to what many people believe, mistreatment of nature is not a recent phenomenon. Moreover, only a little travel in developing countries is necessary to convince anyone that such behavior is not solely a direct by-product of industrialization. Certainly, none of this excuses us from our ludicrous approach to the very systems that keep us alive, but it does pose a provocative question relating directly to the problem of environmental education: What is there about humans that causes us to act so perversely toward the soil, air, water, and other resources upon which we depend for our very existence?

Jacob Bronowski, in *The Ascent of Man,* proposes, "We are nature's unique experiment to make the rational intelligence prove itself sounder than the reflex." If Bronowski is right, then I suggest that things are not going well in the laboratory. Again I ask, Why?

I believe it has to do with *decision making.* More precisely, our treatment of nature directly is related to the structure of the decisions we confront in our daily lives as individuals, business firms, and government entities. By examining decision making, we can find points of entry for environmental education. That is, we can locate those areas of human activity where such education can have its greatest impact.

First, we have *alternatives.* In any decision, we select one alternative from the set of alternatives before us. Second, we have a set of criteria that we apply to the selection of an alternative. Put another way, in decisions of any consequence we are confronted with multiple, but conflicting, criteria that we use as yardsticks in evaluating the relative desirability of the alternatives before us. In my consulting and executive development work, I find the notion of criteria and their role in decision making to be the most elusive and misunderstood concept in managerial thinking. I have no reason to doubt the same is true in the environmental arena.

For example, in purchasing a VCR, people will be concerned with price, service availability, warranty, various technical features of the unit, and so forth. The same problem confronts the Iowa farmer in deciding what agricultural practices to use. The farmer must somehow sort through a confusing set of objectives, including cost, productivity measures, soil conservation, and impact on surface water and groundwater quality. Furthermore, and this is not readily admitted, an important criterion for all but the most self-confident is what the neighbors will think. Certain conservation farming practices, such as no-till, can carry with them high social costs in the form of derisive comments at the local cafe, or at least they have in the past.

Another part of decision making has to do with outcomes. And in complex decisions such as what farming method to use, each alternative implicitly will be assigned a score on each of the criteria relevant to the decision. Thus, filter strips along waterways might score high on the soil conservation criterion but somewhat lower on the potential for groundwater contamination. Summing up the scores of each alternative as measured against each criterion, other things being equal, results in the alternatives ranked in order of preference in terms of their overall outcomes.

The first inclination of people concerned with protecting the environment is to argue their case on the basis of beauty and justice and the magic of nature. In matters of environmental policy, only a little experience is required to discover that beauty and justice and the magic do not sell, particularly when you're confronting highway engineers.

Given that difficulty, the propensity is next to try something more dramatic, to scream: "Don't you see? Can't you understand the importance of caring for the natural systems that sustain us?" I repress that inclination most of the time, for I know that reasonable people will agree such husbandry is important and, forthwith, will return to all the bad habits ravaging the natural environment. And why this perversity? Why, even though they might agree that protecting the environment is important, do people continue their prodigal ways? I think, as I said before, it has to do with decision making.

I wish it were not so. How much easier the tasks of conservation and enhancement of our natural gifts would be if everyone could agree that, yes, beauty and long-run survival are all that matter and that those reasons are justification enough for altering our destructive behavior. But I think it's a much grittier proposition than that, unfortunately. And that means environmental education and environmental policy are going to have to deal with decision making. Let's pursue this a little further using the decision-making model I just sketched.

Environmentalists are fond of calling for the development of an environmental ethic, which amounts to raising the consciousness of people about the importance of treating our environment with more wisdom than we currently do. I am skeptical about such raw efforts, for they do not address at the most pragmatic level the seemingly infinite set of decisions made each and every day affecting the condition of the environment. As I said earlier, you can always get agreement from reasonable people about the importance of dealing with nature in an enlightened fashion, but such agreement doesn't necessarily change behavior. And it's behavioral change that is the goal, presumably, of environmental education and policy.

When we plead with people for them to increase the importance they place on the natural order, what we really are asking is for them to carry out the following five operations:

1. Put the the environment into their set of decision criteria,
2. Rank the environmental criterion/criteria relatively high in the criteria set,
3. Assign the environmental criterion/criteria a large weight relative to the other criteria,
4. Place into their choice set alternatives that will be favored by the environmental criterion/criteria, and
5. Make sure an environmentally beneficial alternative is chosen based on the rankings and weights assigned to the various criteria being used in the decision.

In other words, calls for a higher level of environmental consciousness are really pleas for manipulating a fairly complex set of arrangements in the structure of decisions facing people. So, one purpose of environmental education is attempting to fiddle with the trade-offs involved in complex decision making where multiple objectives are present.

For example, in purchasing automobiles, those of us concerned with the environment prefer that people compare small, efficient cars with large, inefficient cars and choose the smaller one. Yet the top ten automobiles in the Environmental Protection Agency's fuel-efficiency listing account for only 2 percent of the new cars sold in America each year. It's reasonable to ask, then, why people continue to choose large, inefficient automobiles. Obviously, those who purchase the big cars have ranked criteria such as prestige, hauling capacity, comfort, and so forth higher than environmental considerations, not to mention initial purchase cost and maintenance charges. From the viewpoint of environmental education, the task is to change the criteria ranking and to encourage people at least to consider placing smaller cars into their choice sets.

Here's another illustration. Plenty of information is available about the bulk and bacterial effects of disposable diapers on landfills. This information has been widely publicized. Still, Kimberly-Clark reported a 20.2 percent increase in third-quarter income in 1989, stemming mainly from the sale of feminine-care products and Huggies disposable diapers. Apparently, consumers continue to purchase disposable diapers in spite of the knowledge that our landfills are in trouble.

Again, we can ask, Why? And again, we must conclude that matters such as convenience rank higher in the consumer's criteria set than environmental considerations, since washable cloth diapers still are available and presumably are somewhere in the consumer's mind as an option. In terms of

Kimberly-Clark, profit is a high-ranking criterion, as it is with all business firms, and profit outranks the environment in deciding whether or not to continue selling Huggies (aside from environmental matters, the name Huggies makes me want to spit up). Furthermore, and this is something I'll come back to in a moment, Kimberly-Clark lives in a competitive world and has no incentive to stop selling the disposable diapers as long as other firms continue to provide this product.

What I'm saying is this. If you're advocating consciousness-raising for the development of an environmental ethic as a method for improving our environmental situation, part of what you're really doing is asking for a realignment of decision criteria in terms of their rankings and weights.

Incidentally, the only way the entire subject of ethics has ever made any sense to me is to discuss it in the context of real decision making and particularly in terms of what is in the criteria set, how the criteria are ranked, and how the criteria are weighted relative to one another. Without that perspective, discussions of ethics become vague exercises in philosophy and semantics, nothing more.

Along with alternatives and the outcomes assigned to each alternative via their measurement on a set of criteria is the element of *risk*. In its purest state, risk is really a function of three things: personal attitudes, outcomes, and probabilities. As a nation, we are intolerant of ambiguity and almost totally ignorant in the ways of science. Science lives on probabilities. In fact, Heisenberg's famous uncertainty principle concerning the position, velocity, and direction of elementary particles convinces us that our knowledge of the universe inherently must remain uncertain, in spite of Einstein's dictum, "God does not play dice."

When we start dealing with nature as a whole, rather than in the two-variable kinds of problems at which classical physics excels, the level of complexity becomes staggering. In the types of ecological problems we now confront, there are many variables, and these variables are interrelated in subtle and intricate ways, which often prevents the assignment of good probabilities, let alone unqualified prediction.

The result is that, much of the time, we really don't know with any degree of certainty what the impact will be of a particular option on the natural environment. In other words, we may not even be able to assign probabilities because our data are so sparse. Even if solid data are available, numbers can be crunched and interpreted in various ways, yielding different conclusions from the same set of data.

Consider the various forecasts about the warming of the Earth. The best we can do, because of the complexity and uncertainty we confront, is lay out the possibilities in terms of scenarios. For example, Irving Mintzer, of the World Resources Institute, has provided three such scenarios. One is a "base case," in which nations continue as they are in terms of carbon dioxide emissions, with only minimal support for increased energy efficiency and solar research and development, with some serious attention given to the rate of chlorofluorocarbon production. He estimates this will result in a global warming of 4.7°F by the year 2000 and up to 8.5°F by 2030. Mintzer's "worse case" scenario includes encouragement of high-level use of fossil fuels and continued tropical deforestation, with the results being an increase of 12.6°F by 2030 and a 30° jump by 2075.

Mintzer's good news comes in the form of his "slow buildup scenario." Here, he assumes strong international efforts to reduce greenhouse-gas emissions eventually "stabilizing the atmosphere's composition." As part of this, coal, gas, and oil prices are markedly increased, per-capita energy use declines in industrialized countries, and governments actively pursue the development of solar energy. Furthermore, this scenario includes the assumption that the world undertakes massive reforestation efforts. Even if all of these efforts had begun by 1980, by 2075 we still would experience a warming of between 2.5 and 7.6°F, which is still "greater than any experienced during recorded human history."

Mintzer's scenarios are not the only ones available. A few scientists still scratch around with their data and see no particular reason for alarm, though these people steadily are finding themselves in the minority. The most we can say with any amount of assurance right now seems to be the following:

1. We will experience a warming of the earth.
2. The timing and magnitude of this warming are, at the present time, undetermined.

Confronted with the range of possibilities before them and the prevailing public ignorance about the ways of science and probabilistic reasoning and a high intolerance for ambiguity in general, what are people to do? One response, and one that I believe we are seeing in all areas of environmental concern, is that of psychological denial.

People sense that major changes in the natural environment might require considerable sacrifice and changes in lifestyle. Hence, there is a tendency to downplay the potential harm and continue behaving in the same old ways. This tendency is abetted by the unavoidable disagreements within the scientific community about such issues as timing and magnitude of forthcoming events.

When the average citizen sees scientists quarreling among themselves, debating the parameters and variables and data used in sophisticated computer models and expressing their opinions in loosely argued scenarios, plenty of room is left for the individual to assign his or her own rough-hewn probability assessments about the severity of problems.

In terms of risk and the unpleasant prospect of having to make real sacrifices, what this allows is an overly optimistic assessment of outcomes and probabilities by the man or woman on the street, regardless of what the real data may or may not show.

Prudence would counsel different behavior. As an illustration, consider the notion of home insurance. For any given individual, the probability that his or her house will burn down is extremely small. Yet, people pay rather large sums of money each year to insure their property against fire.

If you compute what is called the "expected value" of the two alternatives confronting the homeowner—"insure" and "do not insure"—you will find that, other things being equal, insurance is not a good buy. (Basically, "expected value" is the potential loss or gain of a given alternative multiplied by the probability of the outcome of that alternative.) Why, then, do we buy insurance?

Because our attitudes toward risk are such that we are willing to incur a certain, small loss now, which is the insurance premium, to avoid even the tiny possibility of a large and ruinous loss in the future. In other words, people are risk-averse in this particular situation.

And consider for a moment how the Federal Drug Administration handles new drugs. Exhaustive tests are run, data is collected, and years may pass before a drug is released, even for those drugs applying to only a few people and their afflictions. On the other hand, when it comes to the natural environment, we conduct ourselves in entirely the opposite fashion. We shoot first and ask questions later. Even more perverse, we ask for absolute proof, which often is difficult or impossible to provide, that damage is being done before we issue cease-and-desist orders.

Now, if people are so worried about the loss of their homes and the quality of the medications they consume, why aren't they even more worried about the pollution of their water, the erosion and poisoning of their soil, the waste of their minerals, and the clogging of their atmosphere? In other words, why aren't they extremely risk-averse when it comes to the natural environment? For two reasons, as I see it.

First, there is the psychological denial already mentioned. This attitude results in assigning a low probability to environmental damage or assessing the possible outcome, if it does occur, as not very harmful, or both. There is considerable evidence available to indicate that humans have a propensity for assigning lower-than-warranted probabilities to undesirable outcomes and higher-than-warranted probabilities to things they want to happen. As Adlai Stevenson once said, "Given the choice between disagreeable fact and agreeable fantasy, we will choose agreeable fantasy."

A second reason has to do with what are called "social traps." The classic characterization of one kind of trap was provided by Garrett Hardin in his 1968 article, "The Tragedy of the Commons," and helps to explain why we behave as we do toward the natural environment. It works like this.

Suppose there is a commodity available to all at no perceptible charge, such as the atmosphere. From the viewpoint of any one individual, his or her pollution is an infinitesimal amount of the total pollution. Seen this way, it appears that the cost, for example, of driving a large automobile is nearly zero in terms of its environmental impact. The attitude is, "My little bit of litter doesn't make any difference," which parallels the excuse that many people give for not voting in public elections. Yet it's obvious that if a large number of people behave in that manner, we're going to have problems with CO_2 emissions. That really doesn't matter. From the individual viewpoint, there is plenty of incentive to pollute. I'm sure the same attitude prevailed in the Mycenaean culture as they slashed and burned their forests.

So even if people believe there is a high probability of an undesirable outcome, that fact doesn't necessarily change their behavior as long as the incentives are such that they incur no perceivable cost for that behavior and, on the contrary, receive a considerable benefit for their conduct.

Nature appears to be "free," "out there." The same logic explains why people continue to use disposable diapers and also why Kimberly-Clark does not find it in its best interest to discontinue the sale of such diapers. The firm gains nothing by such action except the unbankable plaudits of the environmental community and, on the other hand, incurs a considerable negative shift in its income statement.

Thus, on top of the criteria problem mentioned earlier, we also have the problems of psychological denial or a true risk-taking attitude toward decision making, particularly when it comes to nature, along with the additional nastiness of the "commons" syndrome.

In long-range matters concerning the environment, we always are being asked to trade off a certain future for the benefits of an uncertain future that we will not live to see and whose benefits we will not experience. The future has never made for good politics. In discussing the global economic dilemma that is now upon us, William Ruckelshaus, former head of the Environmental Protection Agency, put it this way: "It means trying to get a substantial proportion of the world's people to change their behavior in order to (possibly) avert threats that will otherwise (probably) affect a world most of them will never live to see." In my terms, it's hard to stop thinking of ourselves as wayfarers. In a state or a nation with an aging population, I note, the long-run view is even harder to market.

And that's not all. In addition to criteria, alternatives, probabilities, and risk functions, *monetary interest* must be taken into account. Interest rates are the way we handle time in decision making. All decisions, one way or the other, involve future considerations, and certainly those impacting on the natural environment involve the future in significant fashion. So in some way, either informally or formally, in the sense of computing a financial measurement such as present value or an internal rate of return, the time value of our outcomes must be taken into account. And the interest rate attached to various decision situations can be affected in subtle fashion by such things as attitude toward risk or psychological denial.

High discount rates used in computing benefit-cost analyses or in just everyday thinking tend to promote the short term over the long term. Environmentally favored alternatives, such as preservation of wilderness, always seem to suffer when compared with competing projects, such as the building of a dam in a wilderness area. The reason, along with the criteria problem discussed earlier and unduly optimistic probability assessments, has to do with the discount rate used in assessing the relative desirability of the projects.

Even a modest psychological bias favoring economic growth and present satisfactions over long-term environmental protection can result in either overt or covert manipulation of the discount rate used. The higher the rate of interest, the less desirable the environmental projects will appear, since they usually exhibit large initial opportunity costs and benefits that stream in over a long period of time, with the benefits accruing to posterity in most cases.

After this deluge of technical business, let me provide an interim summary. I'm arguing that to make any sense at all of why humans are so destructive of the natural environment, we must approach it from the viewpoint of decision making. Confronted with a set of alternatives, one or more of which are environmentally desirable in a given situation, several things control the choice of an alternative. One of these is the content of the criteria set used in evaluating the alternatives and their projected outcomes. If no criteria relevant to the natural environment are included in this set, no alternative with positive environmental implications will be chosen. Even if such criteria are included in the criteria set, the ranking and weighting of these criteria relative to other criteria such as cost and convenience are critical.

Involved in the ranking of alternatives, in addition to criteria, are matters of risk attitude, probability assignments, and the discount rate used. In short, I'm talking about incentives. If all of this seems a trifle theoretical to you, it should not, for it closely parallels the decision processes used in benefit-cost analyses and by individuals themselves, even though in the latter case the analysis conducted usually is intuitive and implicit.

You have only to look at the history of American agricultural policy and its impact on soil and water to see the power of incentives at work. In the sixty years preceding the Conservation Reserve Program of 1985, virtually every agricultural bill contained built-in incentives to induce soil erosion, and these incentives had a powerful influence on decision making at the level of the individual farmer.

Having said all of that, what are the implications for environmental education? As a beginning, I'll digress by gently pointing out that we tend to see education as a panacea for all of our problems, whether these problems involve drugs or violence or the natural environment. As soon as a problem of virtually any kind arises, you can count on the calls for "more education" to begin. Robert Hutchins, the great philosopher of education, once made the following observation: "To say that education will overcome such and such a problem amounts to saying: 'If we were wise, we would know what to do. The object of education is to make us wise. Therefore, let us have education.' "

Personally, I think such calls are a convenient excuse, in many cases, for delaying action that may require difficult decisions. So does Hutchins, for he also stated:

> One who proclaims salvation through education evades the necessity of doing something about the slums. One who sees education as the

> prime requirement of the poverty-stricken nations does not have to try to keep them from starving. Those who talk of education as the sole means of solving the race problems, or of obtaining lasting peace, or of curing juvenile delinquency, often seem to mean that they have not much interest in these subjects, certainly not much interest in inconveniencing themselves about them.

In other words, education, in some respects, has become a very large closet into which we shunt our problems.

But, given the language of the Iowa Resource Enhancement and Protection (REAP) act, I judge that education is only one part of a much larger commitment to environmental improvement. That, in itself, causes me to take the call for education more seriously than I might otherwise have taken it. So I'll turn next to an exploration of environmental education not only in terms of the decision model I already have presented, but also in some larger frameworks as well.

Obviously, given what I have said about decision making, one task of environmental education is to get environmental concerns into the criteria set that businesses, governments, and individuals employ in their decision making. Unless that occurs, nothing happens. What we're talking about here, really, is knowledge.

The prevailing assumption is that if people truly understand the impact they are having on the environment, then they will behave differently. Maybe, maybe not. I've already shown that even when environmental knowledge is present, such as in the case of disposable diapers, other criteria can dominate environmental sensibilities. A brief stroll around our university campuses will convince you that knowledge and intelligence, if you'll permit me to assume that both of those can be found on our campuses, are not enough. The parking lots are full of large automobiles, until just recently styrofoam cups were everywhere, and the waste of paper is absolutely incredible.

So the task is not only to get the natural environment

into people's criteria set, but also to get environmental criteria highly ranked and weighted in this set. Let me say that I'm a little skeptical about the efficacy of this approach, though I'll readily bow to proof from those who are experts in environmental education, which I'm not. I'm skeptical because of all the reasons I've already mentioned. In general, I believe people respond to concrete incentives more than vague philosophical beliefs. I wish it were not so, but that's what my experience tells me. There are those, of course, who behave now, have behaved in the past, and will behave in the future in responsible fashion toward the environment.

Just why some people will sacrifice in the cause of environmental preservation while others will not is something of a mystery. Looked at another way, a small minority of people have the natural environment as a highly ranked criterion in their decision making and live their lives consistent with good treatment of nature.

Tom Tanner, Professor of Environmental Studies at Iowa State University, conducted research several years ago designed to uncover why some people "strive for the preservation of a habitable, resource-rich planet to pass on to posterity." His conclusions agree exactly with something I argued when I was part of a team looking at environmental education in the 1970s. Tanner says: "I discovered an overwhelmingly clear common pattern: As children, my subjects had spent many hours alone or with a few friends in relatively pristine habitats that were usually accessible every day. The nature of these habitats varied with the settings of the respondents' childhood homes; they included vacant lots, undeveloped city parks, and farmlands." He also notes that studies in Illinois and Maine resulted in similar conclusions.

Those of you who have read more of my writings, particularly my pieces on the Shell Rock River, know that I spent exactly the sort of boyhood Tanner is describing. There is something about that kind of early experience that sticks the natural environment into your mind and into your decision criteria.

The problem comes in providing that kind of environment for all children. Unfortunately, the increasing urbanization of America along with the competition from television and other distractions seems to work against it. Like Tanner, I have doubts about the efficacy of standard classroom instruction, occasional field trips, or brief outdoor camping experiences as methods of creating environmental awareness at a level where the individual's decision processes will be profoundly influenced.

Tanner, by the way, suggests authorized "hooky" days where students are allowed to roam relatively pristine natural areas with only loose supervision. He even proposes, in jest, something called the Huck Finn Elementary School, named after the famous truant. I think that's where I went to school, as my mother, I'm sure, would testify.

President Jimmy Carter's call for energy conservation as something like the environmental equivalent of war went unheeded in the 1970s. People just went out and bought more big automobiles, as far as I could tell. When gas prices began to climb, however, people responded by buying smaller cars. At the present, as is so often the case, our incomes are once again outrunning the price of gasoline, and the return to large vehicles and high-performance engines has occurred. There is something important in this phenomenon, and it has to do with cost as an incentive or disincentive, depending on how you wish to view it.

Education can help push the natural environment into our criteria sets, but not at the same level of intensity as what I call the two C's—cost and crisis. Both of those grab people's attention and get the natural environment high up into their criteria sets.

Crisis, however, is what we seek to avoid, even though we are not very successful at it. A major reason has to do with the inability of the market economy to reflect the true costs of doing business, particularly when these are environmental costs. This is a long and well-known argument, so I will not belabor it here. Suffice it to say, when prices of products do not reflect their true costs, we overproduce and overconsume them. That's the cost part of the two C's.

I can assure you that if the price of gasoline reflected its true costs, and that might be at $2 to $3 a gallon currently, we would see a rapid decrease in the rate of CO_2 emissions. Why? Because, and this is my own notion, the natural environment has now entered the criteria set as a proxy in the form of cost—it has sneaked in through the back door, so to speak. That is, because of cost, people will be making environmentally responsible decisions even though the natural environment was not even in their conscious minds.

Cost, except for the very rich, ordinarily is an important criterion in all decisions. The trick is, then, to get cost to reflect environmental concerns. And this is a key role for environmental education that is not often recognized. We tend to think of such education as focused on the young, but the people who really need it, when it comes to incentives and criteria, are those who pass laws and administer them. My contention is that the use of incentives is one of the poorly understood facets of modern policymaking.

When a problem presents itself, the least creative response is to pass a law preventing undesirable behaviors. Granted, that's sometimes the only response. But laws require policing of one kind or another. Far better is the search for how incentives might be manipulated in such a way that people make the correct decisions without any policing and, in fact, without really thinking about environmental ethics at all. As biologist David Ehrenfeld says: "I believe that the ultimate success of all conservation will depend on a revision of the way we use the world in our everyday living when we are not thinking about conservation. If we have to conserve the Earth in spite of ourselves, we will not be able to do it." I happen to agree with that statement.

One of the best instruments of social policy ever invented in this country was the Individual Retirement Account, which, like all good ideas, got the ax. It had just about everything going for it. It provided a powerful incentive to save for the long run by providing a short-term benefit in the form of a tax credit. This took care of two things without any government intervention. First, it was a way of encouraging people to save for their later years, while making them feel good about doing it. Second, it increased the savings pool and, hence, the capital available for investment.

Politicians, in the mid-1980s stampede to cut taxes, argued that the tax system should not be an instrument of social policy. That's nonsense. Taxes are one of the few powerful and yet surgical ways the government has of influencing private decision making. The IRAs were a method of bringing the future back to the present, and we need a great deal more decision structures that do exactly that.

Therefore, one of the most important roles that any environmental educator can play is to educate those in positions of power about the appropriate use of incentives. In addition, while they're doing that, the educators also can deal with the issues of probability, how scientific knowledge is generated and what the current findings really say, and the choice of appropriate discount rates in projects involving the natural environment. In short, we're talking about adult education of a fairly sophisticated kind, not just field trips and classroom presentations for junior high school students.

I'll stay with this notion of cost for a little while longer and link it to the ideas I discussed earlier about risk, since the constructive use of cost is absolutely crucial to getting us on track environmentally. In formal decision theory, there is something called the *pessimist's criterion.* What this amounts to is really a decision rule that proposes the following conservative approach: In any situation, if good probability estimates are not available, figure out what the worst possible outcomes are and select an alternative that assures you the best possible results if the worst set of circumstances comes to pass.

Now, if you live your whole life that way, and if a state or nation or business conducts all its affairs that way, life would not only be boring, but also would grind to a halt. Taking risks is a part of forging ahead. But, in thinking about the natural systems that sustain life on this planet, the pessimist approach has some merit. Surely, it's the criterion we invoke in deciding whether or not to insure our homes and whether or not a new drug should be approved.

It seems, therefore, the conservative point of view always would be correct when survival is at stake. Yet we behave in almost exactly the opposite fashion, as I pointed out earlier. We invoke what is called the "optimist's criterion," which states that, when good probability estimates are absent, assume the best of all possible worlds will prevail and act accordingly. Implicitly, this is the way we have dealt with the natural environment.

The point is this: Even though we may be optimists about the capacity of the natural environment to absorb whatever punishments we may hand out, the use of cost as a disincentive to environmental damage is just a way of making a moderate pessimist out of a Pollyanna. Even though the optimism may still be there, cost as a disincentive is acting to produce conservative behavior. Gasoline at $3 a gallon would create changes in behavior that have nothing to do with beliefs about probabilities, risk, and the importance of the natural environment.

In addition to working on criteria, environmental education must also provide *alternatives* for decision makers. It's not enough to have the natural environment as an important component of a criteria set; you must also have alternatives that, if chosen, will result in environmentally constructive outcomes.

This is a major weakness in the current state of environmental education. Partly because of publicity forecasting substantial sacrifice in the short term, partly because of costs that already have arrived, and partly, let's say, because of good conscience, we have arrived at what people in education like to call "the teachable moment." We have the public's attention, to some extent.

But the public, including myself, asks: "Okay, what can I do? What are my alternatives?" For example, how can I help organize and participate in a recycling program. Let me propose a project that will bring the state of Iowa a landslide of good publicity, as well as benefit the natural environment. We should produce a simple, easy-to-use publication called "A Handbook for Sustainable Living" and distribute this handbook to every Iowa household. If we do this, I assure you that every state in the nation, and probably other countries, will be banging on our door for copies. We'll sell the book at a modest profit, pay back the costs of producing it, and plow the rest back into more environmental education, all the while doing a considerable favor to the natural environment and enhancing the image of Iowa.

Along these lines, Les Kaufman, a practical, tough-minded biologist, has made an accurate observation about public television shows dealing with nature. He says this:

Although nature spectaculars attract a large audience, most regular viewers of public television are seasoned converts to the environmental way of thinking. These people should by now be receiving a different, more sophisticated message that producers are, for the most part, failing to provide. Too often, nature and science shows offer a fare that is predictable and sophomoric. Afficionados of public television have come to expect every natural history film to end with a cacophony of chainsaws, bulldozers, fishing fleets, and wild animal collectors busily desecrating nature as the announcer solemnly intones his final moralistic monologue.

Kaufman is exactly right.

And, as we get our handbook together, let's also commandeer, if that's the right word, Iowa Public Television for an evening, lay out the problems before us, and offer the audience some rich alternatives for leading more environmentally sensitive lives. That would be another first. No exhortations, no droning explanations about the biology of marshlands and our geological history. None of that, not this time. Just good solid analysis of the problems and practical day-to-day solutions that people can implement without government grants. Hell, maybe we even can peddle the tape to other states and make a buck doing that as well.

Furthermore, we also need to show people that by spending ourselves into environmental oblivion, we are decreasing the options available to us. Proponents of economic growth are fond of talking about expanding choices. But, as the economist E. J. Mishan has pointed out, at the same time that we are rolling the carpet of increased choice out in front of us, we also are rolling it up behind us in terms of resource depletion, pollution, and the like. Whenever we open a forest to serious logging or build a dam in a wilderness valley or burn another ton of coal, we are decreasing the options open to us in the future. Again, it's a matter of cost and bringing the future back to the present.

Earlier I mentioned "the teachable moment." Though I think a minority, possibly a substantial one, of people are ready to learn about environmental responsibility, I'm not certain they are ready to *sacrifice* for it. In spite of having the most elaborate set of environmental regulations in the world, Americans have not been asked to give up very much in either money or lifestyles to support environmental protection.

Iowa is somewhat of an oasis in this regard. Through the REAP act and the 1987 groundwater bill, we have stated rather clearly that we are prepared to make sacrifices, real financial commitments, on behalf of the natural environment over the long run. Other states are beginning to think this way also.

So, even though the teachable moment may be here, I'm doubtful that most people are willing to put their money and their convenience on the line, and that's what we're all going to be asked to do. Those in the hazardous waste business are fond of quoting the NIMBY principle—Not In My Back Yard. Just as difficult is what I have labeled the NIMBA principle, which means Not In My Bank Account (remember you read it here first). The tendency, I fear, will be to look for the easy technological fix rather than sacrificing.

Beyond decision making, and yet related to it, are a number of other functions of environmental education, not all of them popular. One area that will be a little dicey politically is the head-on collision between the push for economic development and environmental quality. The major contribution to be made here by environmental educators is to help people to see that economics and ecology are intertwined, even though we have treated them as divorced in the past. (We even have separate courses in our universities in environmental economics, which amounts to separating that which cannot be separated.)

You cannot talk about economics without talking about the natural environment. It's that simple. One action that must be taken immediately is to form close organizational ties among the Department of Natural Resources, the Department of Economic Development, and the Department of Transportation. There are various ways of doing this, such as project management, overlapping committees, and people who serve as linking pins between the various departments.

Then there are our automobiles. If 125 people attend a governor's conference on the environment and they average a two-hundred-mile round-trip in getting there and getting back home, at twenty-five miles per gallon of gasoline, they will have put ten thousand pounds of CO_2 into the atmosphere by their attendance. Under the same assumptions, the atmospheric tab for a University of Iowa football game is around five and a half million pounds of CO_2, just for the spectators. That's about the equivalent of twelve hundred autos driven for an entire year. Or, how about stock car racing and trips to the regional shopping mall and demolition derbies and family vacations and business trips and tractor pulls and something called "Big Foot" that crunches cars in the UNI-Dome once or twice a year?

My suspicion is that the environmental education folks would rather leave these problems to the price system rather than arguing for out-and-out prohibition. In fact, I'd recommend it. But remember that there are approximately five hundred million automobiles registered on this planet, each with an average fuel consumption of two gallons per day, and at the current rate of increase, there will be two billion autos by 2025. Those figures alone are enough to keep anyone awake at night.

Another area of frustration will be the impatience we tend to exhibit as a culture. The classic statement I hear constantly in all problem arenas is, "Let's get it solved and put it behind us." As an executive at one of the largest industrial empires in America recently said to me when I finished describing the global environmental situation to him: "Okay, tell me what to do and I'll do it. Let's get on with the problem solving and get it over with." And recently, when my wife mentioned the greenhouse effect, a woman replied: "All we have to do is stop using hair spray."

Thus, there will be a tendency on the part of Americans to treat the environmental crisis approaching us like the Second World War—crank up the scientists, rev up industry, mobilize the troops, and let's get going. Unfortunately, the environmental dilemma is a lot more like the Vietnam War, full of frustration and uncertainty and ambiguity and enduring sacrifice, with no end in sight, because there is no end.

In the school systems, environmental education confronts an overloaded schoolday, at least in the eyes of the teachers. We're busy training our children how to become good little partners in economic growth, and there's not much room left for the environment. Fifteen years ago, I suggested we piggyback environmental education onto every other subject, since the environment figures into everything we do, from breathing on up.

To illustrate the feasibility of this, I rewrote an existing eighth-grade mathematics textbook so that each mathematical concept was taught using a problem from the natural environment instead of using trivial puzzles such as how many pizzas can be bought with such and such amount of money. It can be done, not just in mathematics, but in all fields; it's not that hard. And it provides an angle of entry for environmental education into already burdened curriculums.

To sum up, in general, somebody's got to start talking seriously and hard to people about the ominous possibilities just over the horizon from us. If the greenhouse effect comes to pass, and the evidence certainly points in that direction, or even if it doesn't, we're going to have some serious social problems involving food, water, and air, not to mention matters of everyday civility and public health. We tend to get overconfident about our place in this world and forget such things as the nasty fact that world food stocks in August of 1988 were down to 218 million metric tons—enough to last forty-seven days. That's not much slack.

Moreover, there are profound theological questions yet to be addressed as we influence nature to greater and greater extremes. Bill McKibben discusses this in *The End of Nature.*

At the beginning of this essay, I said that we have treated nature as "out there," and in that very way we also have found the existence of God, in terms of seeing nature as His handiwork. If we now have subsumed nature as part of the human enterprise, what does that say about God?

We are parties to events that may well result in the greatest changes humans have ever confronted, greater even than the agricultural revolution and the industrial revolution. Before us is a set of problems that are interlocked, complex, and dangerous, scientifically, socially, and theologically:

—Warming of the earth

—Problems with the ozone layer

—Extinction of species. Most ecologists believe we are in the midst of the greatest mass extinction of species in our history.

—Water. Our water supplies are both polluted and disappearing.

—Soil. Lester Brown of the Worldwatch Institute, and many others think the situation is serious. Others are more optimistic.

—Food. This has not been a problem, except for the tragic distribution problems, mostly political, in countries such as Ethiopia. However, the optimistic forecasts I have read fail to take into account the potential effects on growing conditions of the greenhouse effect and the decrease in biological diversity.

—Population. Some people put this at the top of the list and see it as the major cause of all our environmental woes.

That's one way to look at it. Another view deals with per capita consumption and that's a problem of culture as much as population.

—Fossil fuels. Our fossil fuels are running out. There's no question about that. Our known reserves of natural gas are about forty years at present rates of consumption. Those proposing nuclear energy as the fix to this problem have, I believe, not thought through the economics and environmental consequences of this substitution very carefully.

—Trash and hazardous waste disposal. Garbage and hazardous waste are accumulating everywhere, and landfills are closing. We have six thousand landfills now but are heading toward only two thousand in the next few years. Recycling will be of considerable help here in many instances, but certainly not all. Energy cannot be reused, and the pollutants from our fossil fuels certainly can be classified as hazardous wastes.

In sum, while worrying about financial deficits, we have run and are running up ecological deficits that dwarf the financial deficits. As Lester Thurow put it: "No one inherited more wealth than we. We are not the poor boy who worked his way to the top, but the little rich boy who inherited a vast fortune."

We are in the process of squandering this vast fortune. And standing on the other side of the window watching us do it, their faces pressed against the glass, are nearly four billion people in the less-developed countries who now, and rightly so, want a piece of the good life, as world population heads toward nine or ten billion in the next forty years. That's a haunting image to dwell upon.

Basically, as I have argued, I think we're going to have to deal with all of this through the structure of decisions confronting people and firms and governments in their day-to-day decision making.

REAP is a start. A big start. Iowans have been no less guilty in their treatment of nature than anyone else. The difference is we are prepared to atone for our sins. Using this program wisely, we can become the model for the world on how to function as an enlightened, advanced civilization, living with nature rather than dominating it. I always have thought it curious that we need a separate word—environmentalist—to describe those of us concerned about nature. You'd think, since we all depend upon the natural environment for survival, that we'd all be environmentalists and such a word would be redundant.

The fact that there is a separate group of people called environmentalists, who are relatively unpopular in many quarters, merely illustrates our degree of alienation from nature. REAP and Iowa and efforts of concerned citizens can go a long way toward making the label "environmentalist" truly redundant, forever obsolete. To be a citizen of the planet Earth should be reason enough to be an environmentalist, and that point of view ultimately is the task of environmental education.

Robert James Waller grew up in Rockford, Iowa, and was educated at the University of Northern Iowa and Indiana University. He has taught management at the University of Northern Iowa since 1968, and from 1979 to 1986 he served as dean of UNI's College of Business. He has lectured and published widely in the fields of problem solving and decision making and has worked as a consultant to business corporations and governmental institutions throughout the United States and around the world. Waller also has performed extensively as a singer and a guitarist, starred in basketball at the high school and college levels, and is a serious photographer who travels Iowa and the world for his photographic images.